THE SIGNET CLASSIC POETRY SERIES is under the general editorship of poet, lecturer, and teacher JOHN HOLLANDER.

Mr. Hollander's first volume of poetry, *A Crackling of Thorns,* won the Yale Series of Younger Poets Award for 1958. He was a recipient of a National Institute of Arts and Letters grant (1963) and has been a member of the Wesleyan University Press Poetry Board and the Bollingen Poetry Translation Prize Board. Mr. Hollander is Professor of English at Hunter College.

Selected Poetry of Marvell is edited by critic, author, and teacher FRANK KERMODE. Mr. Kermode is Professor of English at the University of Bristol, England. He was Flexner Lecturer at Bryn Mawr College in the United States and formerly held the John Edward Taylor Professorship of English Literature at the University of Manchester, England. Professor Kermode has lectured at the universities of Durham and Reading in England, and was Warton Lecturer at the British Academy (1962). He is the editor of the Signet Classic edition of *The Winter's Tale* and of the Arden edition of *The Tempest.* His books include *John Donne, Romantic Image, The Living Milton, Wallace Stevens,* and *The Sense of an Ending.* Mr. Kermode is an editor of *Encounter* magazine.

Andrew Marvell

SELECTED POETRY

Edited by Frank Kermode

The Signet Classic Poetry Series
GENERAL EDITOR: JOHN HOLLANDER

PUBLISHED BY
THE NEW AMERICAN LIBRARY, NEW YORK AND TORONTO
THE NEW ENGLISH LIBRARY LIMITED, LONDON

First Printing, June, 1967

Library of Congress Catalog Card Number: 67-25582

SIGNET TRADEMARK REG. U.S. PAT. OFF. AND FOREIGN COUNTRIES
REGISTERED TRADEMARK—MARCA REGISTRADA
HECHO EN CHICAGO, U.S.A.

SIGNET CLASSICS are published *in the United States* by
The New American Library, Inc.,
1301 Avenue of the Americas, New York, New York 10019,
in Canada by The New American Library of Canada Limited,
295 King Street East, Toronto 2, Ontario,
in the United Kingdom by The New English Library Limited,
Barnard's Inn, Holborn, London, E.C. 1, England

PRINTED IN THE UNITED STATES OF AMERICA

Contents

Introduction

When Marvell died in 1678, the government was considering an informer's report which named him as the author of *An Account of the Growth of Popery*. The report was correct, and the informer said nothing that was not widely known. At the time of the poet's death all the talk must have been of this and similar works which attacked the deviousness of the King, and his failure to prevent his brother from plotting a French papist takeover in England. Marvell was the satirist, the controversialist, expert in the joint territories of politics and religion; he was the classical republican, sketching in advance the principles of 1688, and an eighteenth-century man before his time. His epitaph in St. Giles grants him "wit and learning, with a singular penetration and strength of judgment," but whereas we should use these words of the poet, the writer of the tribute thought of him almost exclusively as a patriot politician. When his *Miscellaneous Poems* appeared in 1681, they attracted little attention, though his satirical fame was great, and people thought him the author of a considerable body of anti-establishment writing with which he had had nothing to do.

Satirical and topical writing, unless of the highest class, loses its hold in a generation. Marvell's did well, partly because of his posthumous reputation for political integrity. He stood for freedom and toleration (except in the case of Romanists) and for gentlemanly patriotism under, at most, a constitutional monarch. In the eighteenth century, the opposition party, whether Whig or Tory, tended to treat him as an exemplary ancient hero. And in a major edition of 1776 the lyric and pastoral poetry appear to have been included merely for the sake of completeness.

All this was to change, though slowly. To Wordsworth, Marvell was the republican friend of Milton, one of the "great men" who "have been among us." But Lamb admired the "witty delicacy" of *The Garden* and *The Nymph Complaining,* and in the succeeding century the emphasis was quite altered. One landmark is the large edition of Grosart (1872), another, following the late Victorian revival of interest in seventeenth-century poetry which Grosart helped to bring about, is T. S. Eliot's tercentenary essay of 1921.[1] This provided us with a critical terminology of which the use is not yet exhausted; there is a sensitivity to the text and a profound historical perspective characteristic of Eliot at his best; he largely determined the shape of our understanding of a poet now thought to be of major status.

The matter of historical perspective is important. Immediately behind Marvell stand some very good poets, whose work he knew well: Jonson, Carew, Lovelace, Randolph. He understood the older world, could respond easily to the comprehensiveness as well as to the novelty of Milton; but he was an exact contemporary of Cowley, who of all English poets probably best deserves the epithet "transitional," and suffered most from his own awareness of its justice. But to relate Marvell myopically to such poets as these is in the end misleading, and the neat close work of literary history has usually done him harm. He has often been labeled a member of the "school of Donne"; yet he is obviously not like Donne. His metric belongs to a different tradition; he is less argumentative, less dedicated to the "strong line"; he offers, as Donne never does, and yet quite otherwise than Carew or Lovelace, a blend of English wit and European *acutezza;* his wit, as Lamb saw, has more delicacy, and his strength is altogether less a matter of strenuously devious argument and colloquial verve, than those of any other poet. Furthermore, within the limits of

---

[1] For a satisfactory and accessible account of the history of Marvell's reputation, see Legouis, cap. viii.

his enterprise, he is more various both in theme and in tone than any poet of the period except, perhaps, Jonson.

In short, one needs a longer historical perspective and a deeper one, such as Eliot sketched in his essay. "Marvell's best verse is the product of European, that is to say Latin, culture," Eliot remarked; and from this culture derive his *wit* and his *magniloquence*. The poet's wit is memorably described as "a tough reasonableness beneath the slight lyric grace"; playing over "the great traditional common-places of European literature," it renews them. The impact of this individual talent on the tradition refreshes its order, and touches off in us (who belong still to that civilization) resonances of civility, order and passion such as only poetry organized within a valid historical culture can stir. Thus Marvell takes "a slight affair, the feeling of a girl for her pet, and gives it a connexion with that inexhaustible and terrible nebula of emotion which surrounds all our exact and practical passions and mingles with them . . ." The poet's intelligence and imagination, working on the inexhaustible resonances of the Latin tradition, establishes the necessary "equipoise, a balance and proportion of tones"; it finds "the proper degree of seriousness for every subject" and confers upon it "wit's internal equilibrium."

These phrases may remind the reader of what Marvell criticism ought to be, and of the directions, the necessary discretions and discriminations, that more extensive criticism ought to pursue and develop. To study him is to study not so much a personal quality, not even a literary quality, but "a quality of a civilisation."

This does not mean, of course, that nothing can usefully be said of his personal quality. As a political thinker, Marvell was an innovating traditionalist, independently intelligent but close to the best that was thought and said; a dissenter whose dissidence was not rancorous, and one who accepted political and religious variations without ceasing to be his own man. Sympathetic to the King and to the "ancient rights," he accepted Cromwell; believing, as he remarked later, that "the Cause was too good to have been fought for"—meaning that the success of Parliament was of historical necessity, and that this history needed no midwife—he acknowledged the Protector as a soldier monarch who not only ruined one great work of time but founded another. As a commentator on the state, Marvell experienced tensions of interest and reference very similar to those more directly presented in his poetry; they proceed from the collision between a novel present and great but variable historical structures, institutional and ideological. We are dealing with that incessantly changing thing, the "quality of a civilisation"; a remarkable and inclusive intelligence records the conflict between old model and new experience, finds a rhetoric, balanced and serious, to vindicate the attempt and to express as well as to resolve the strains. The agents of such poetry, wit and magniloquence, are themselves products of the civility which is their subject.

Almost half a century has passed since Eliot's essay, and, with a few exceptions, the critics have done nothing to implement it. They prefer easier tasks, such as devising essentially simple equations (obscured by the cloudy prose of inferior historians-of-ideas) between poems and "contemporary thought"—notably, nowadays, between Marvell's poems and Cambridge Platonism. This practice is often made worse by a desire to establish in a body of poems some essential unity of idea, so that any poem (for example, *To his Coy Mistress*) which ostensibly violates that unity becomes the occasion for some vain exegetical epicycle. Obviously we must understand that the presiding personality of the poet—of which we certainly have a strong sense—is not to be thus determined, and allow for the fact that the vitality of the poems derives in part from the traditions to which they indirectly assert their relation, traditions which, on a myopic view, may seem mutually contradictory. They belong to the history of poetry, considered as an aspect of the history of civility, rather than to a temporary arrangement of ideas; and to read them one needs to give some weight to what is specific in them, to the poetic attitudes which they allude to and transform. Though they share the qualities of "wit and learning, with a singular penetration and strength of judgment," they ask of the critic a respect for their relationship to traditions not invented by the poet, and not to be resolved in some generalization about his thought; his penetration and judgment must respect, in this sense, their singularity. Consequently, the remainder of this introduction will consist of a piecemeal handling of some of the poems; sketchy as they necessarily are, these notes will avoid any suggestion that there is in Marvell some time-bound, specious "unity of thought."

AN HORATIAN ODE

This poem has fared better than any other at the hands of recent critics. The palpable complexity of political reference has, I suppose, prevented oversimplification. The powerful sense of *control* is attributed to a rhetorical mastery of ambiguous material; the poet who speaks the *Ode* is, we feel, a master whose strenuous balance is that of an intellectual athlete, fully coordinated, leaning on the wind of history; and it so happens that the story of Marvell's political thought allows us to make a partial identification of the poet with him. At the center of the *Ode,* we might say, is a point where the horizontal and the vertical of history cross. It is early summer, 1650, between Cromwell's return from Ireland in May, and his departure for Scotland in July. It is also a moment in what might be called imperial historiography: the imitations of Lucan are intended to bring to bear on the contemporary history the great crisis caused by Caesar's violation of ancient rights, his casting the archetypal state into another mold, and his role as dictator or protector. (It was not Caesar but Pompey who at that time lost his head.) The imitation of Horace reminds us of the force which accompanies the overthrow and establishment of empire. The political and poetical resonances are consonant here; the material of the *Ode* is in part the reverberant events of 1649 and 1650, but it is also imperial history, with its real and its mythical perspectives.

To the resulting complexities some modern critics have done justice, from Cleanth Brooks in 1946 to John M. Wallace in 1962. All have to deal with certain puzzling

facts. In 1648 Marvell wrote the prefatory lines to Love-
lace's *Lucasta,* and perhaps the elegy on Francis Villiers,
which show him to have had strong Royalist sympathies.
More remarkably, *Tom May's Death,* written a few
months *after* the *Ode,* is also Royalist in tone. Not much
more than a year later Marvell was a member of the
household of a retired Parliamentary general (though
Fairfax had not approved the execution of the King, or
the preventive war against Scotland); by 1653 he was
employed by Cromwell, and in the following year wrote
the panegyrical *First Anniversary.* Brooks's insistence
that we read the poem and not Marvell's mind is often
approved of but usually ignored. Are we to imagine a
speaker totally uncommitted, as some suggest? Or a tough
mind that may express only in order to shed a certain
regret for the ancient rights and the noble victim? Hardly,
as Brooks says: the poem is passionately *interested,* con-
scious of the grandeur and pregnancy of the moment. Its
ambiguities are not those of indifference, though they are
undoubtedly present: the poem circulated surreptitiously
among Royalists at the time of its writing, though their
descendants took steps to prevent its publication in 1681.

The poem has been called Machiavellian, praising a
Machiavellian prince; even Clarendon, who thought Crom-
well "a brave bad man," admitted that he "totally declined
Machiavells methode," but Marvell could after all have
been wrong about this, as he was about Cromwell's part
in Charles's flight to Carisbrooke. Certainly the *Ode*
seems to say, what everybody knew to be Machiavelli's
belief, that what men do is more important than what
they ought to do, that things are as they are and not as
we would have them. Mr. Wallace, declining this view,
argues that the poem is designed on the plan recommended
by rhetoricians for a deliberative speech intended to sway
a doubtful audience—in other words, its dubieties about
Cromwell, its concessive tone ("And, if we would speak
true . . ."), and the excursus on the last moments of the
King are merely rhetorical feints. Marvell's mind was made
up, committed to the new order, condoning the crossing
of the Rubicon; perhaps the means was wicked, but God

sometimes works by such means, as when Samson married Delilah, so as to pull down the Philistian pillars.

Mr. Wallace tries, by dividing the rhetoric of the poem from its poetry, to find a reason for our habitual mistaking of the situation as he sees it. But for all that he says about the deliberative structure, he cannot show its dependence upon a mind made up; poems are written to find out, and what is found out is not a simple intellectual tenet. The *Ode* has its suasive aspect, no doubt; but without severing it from immediate issues of political allegiance and stability one can say that it transcends time, contemplating not only political events but politics more abstractly: ancient rights as against "Fate," the leader as servant of the people, the relevance of modern Machiavellianism and of the myths and commonplaces of imperial history. Wallace documents several such commonplaces.

> The same arts that did gain
> A power must it maintain

is not original in Marvell, but a piece of political realism dating back to Sallust, and commonplace political sagacity in Renaissance statecraft. In the same way, it can be shown that the semi-paradoxical eulogy of Cromwell—he "does both act and know," and is fit "to sway / That can so well obey"—has a history almost as long as that of political and moral speculation. The Cromwell of 1650—regicide, supreme military leader emerged from rural obscurity to ruin the great work of time—is fashioned to fit the myth of the strong retired man who saves the state, like Scipio Africanus. The tinge of millennialism in the concluding section (well identified by Wallace) relates Cromwell not only to the chiliastic mood of his time, but to the Emperor of the Last Days in millennialist mythology. High intelligence confronts a great topic and sees it in historical depth—in terms of an imperial culture; a new situation is related, without loss of local ironies, to the history of a civilization with which it must, in the end, be reconciled.

This is what makes *An Horatian Ode,* on a broad view of its method, resemble the other poems. It defines the range and assurance of Marvell's invention. Thus he probably "invented" the stanza of the *Ode,* but what immediately impresses us about this novelty is that of all English stanzas it most perfectly recalls the public poetry of Horace. Horace is guide, not commander; the tone of the great Actium ode fluctuates cunningly, but it is not so various as Marvell's, though Marvell remembered from it the imagery of hawk and dove, and the muted praise of Cleopatra at the end. An assault on the state, and its reestablishment in a new form, are the subjects of both poets. But Marvell glances back from Augustus to Julius; Cromwell too is a force like one of nature's, which ambiguously but uncontrollably blasts Caesar's head (for if Charles I is the imperial descendant of Caesar, Cromwell is his political descendant). Why, asks Marvell, can it be said that something is due to such a man, so irresistibly destructive? The answer is that he fits the traditional pattern of heroism, as Milton, in the *Second Defense,* said he did (he used the same pattern for Christ in *Paradise Regained*). But Marvell does not merely slide into another rhetorical topic. He makes the rustic life of the hero matter for verse of witty delicacy, and moves, in a grand crescendo, to a sure magniloquence:

> Who, from his private gardens, where
> He lived reservèd and austere,
>   As if his highest plot
>   To plant the bergamot,
> Could by industrious valor climb
> To ruin the great work of Time,
>   And cast the kingdom old
>   Into another mold . . .

And this, he adds in a new modulation, whether we would have it so or not; to protest is merely to be fretful, as if about the weather. The cool tribute to Cromwell's cunning melts into the conscious and solemn complexity of the passage on the King's execution; the theatrical puns hint at something grandly obsolete in the moving spectacle (there had been no real "tragic scaffold" for almost a decade; and later Marvell pointed out that Cromwell was a tragic hero who died the modern way, in bed)—something artificially fine in the King's demeanor, *non humilis* like Horace's Cleopatra, nothing common. . . . The pathos of the passage is torn open by the drumroll immediately succeeding: "This was that memorable hour / Which first assured the forced power." We are out of the theater again; the execution was after all not memorable for the King's behavior, but because it assured the forced power. His head was comely, but more important, it was a good omen for the new state. The tone changes over and over again, to the end, where eulogy blends with admonition. "Equipoise, a balance and proportion of tones . . ."; or, the quality of a civilization. In the light of such a poem even the strong-minded Marvell of the Restoration polemics may seem overcommitted to the local and temporary situation. So, possibly, was the prose Marvell of 1650, or any such that we may seek behind the poem itself.

THE MOWER

We should not, then, look for straight equivalences between the poems and the general set of one man's mind; and when the poems lack so direct a relation to known contemporary events our caution should be greater. We can say, perhaps, that the use of imperial example suggests a civilized power to invent, and to stabilize by wit, new relevance in ancient topics. As an example of topical allusion and renovation, consider *The Mower against Gardens,* which depends upon the sharing between author and reader of a reasonably well-defined area of reference, upon which oblique allusion may construct new patterns.

Originality, in the poetry of the period, is usually a matter of modernizing the known; the conceit is an instrument for adapting old situations to surprising new use; one should make one's thoughts shine—*faire briller ses pensées,* said Saint-Amant, a French poet who had some affinities with Marvell. This is not quite the same as expressing in a new way "what oft was thought"; it rather implies an imaginative review of whole clusters of thoughts immemorially associated, and the discovery of new patterns in them. M. Legouis is uncharacteristically wide of the mark when he says that in *The Mower against Gardens* Marvell "follows no tradition"; the poem relates to an extensive cluster of garden ideas and images.

The complaint against luxury in gardens is ancient and so is the association between them and art, considered as an unnatural tampering with nature, an intrusion of corrupt human interest into the pure creation. On the other hand, gardens were emblematic of beneficent art, restoring the ruins of the first Eden; and art could be a handmaid of nature, just as the garden, for some a place of debauch, could be the scene of virtuous or, indeed, ecstatic meditation. If you spoke up for the pleasures afforded by gardens to the senses you were in accord with Genesis, where the Greek translation gives *paradeisos,* a pleasure garden, and the Vulgate *paradisus voluptatis,* a paradise of pleasure, in which the unfallen parents were as Milton describes them, "to all delight of human sense exposed." But innocently to reenact such voluptuous scenes in a fallen world is beyond a mortal's share; and gardens were often, over the centuries, represented—either with delight or disgust—as granting a license for sexual behavior on a good old primitive pattern. Or it might be said: art goes too far. More natural gardens are instruments of the interior life, mirrors in which to see nature writ small, convenient editions of the Book of the Creatures; if art corrupts the species, Perdita's complaint against gillivors, then this function is betrayed. The pleasures of solitude merge with the sins of sloth. And so on: many variations could be woven round these inherent antitheses, and many figures attached themselves in poems: nature imitating art, fecundity expressed by the importunity of the fruit as it presses on hand or mouth, the wickedness of grafting, the power of the garden to provide the means whereby its inhabitant can transcend the little world it offers and elevate his mind above nature. . . . All

these are ancient themes and may as well be set down
randomly as above, since one supposes all such types to
have been simultaneously present in the minds of author
and audience.

Marvell here is undoubtedly thinking of specific
attacks on great houses and their luxurious gardens.
Horace has one such; and there is a rhetorical exercise of
Papirius Fabianus, reported by Seneca the Elder, which
Marvell presumably knew, since it complains that such
houses include streams and woods within the buildings,
and speaks of "fake" or "enforced" woods, *mentita
nemora.* Papirius also complains that the rich enclose the
fields and prefer imitations to the real thing. Such people,
he says, are like children whose minds are too tiny for
them to appreciate anything they cannot pick up and hug.
They are animated by a disgust for the natural. Here is
the archetype, perhaps, of the topic Marvell chose for
The Mower against Gardens. Given the tradition, it could
well be treated by a man who elsewhere praised the things
he now condemns. But in handling it, a poet will probably
remember that the grafting operations of gardeners are
an image of sexuality, benign or malignant according
to one's stance. He will recall, with wonder or disgust,
Pliny's fabulously productive fruit tree, which as a result
of grafting brought forth annually as much as a whole
orchard in the past—Pliny mentions that this is "adultery."
He also describes a tree at Tivoli which by grafting (a
trick, presumably) bore all kinds of fruit—grapes, pome-
granates, apples, pears, figs, nuts, berries: a splendid
instance of the adulteries of art, or, if you prefer, the
artist's skill in improving nature.

Such ambiguities are the very history of the topic:
throughout, there is an association between gardens and
erotic behavior as well as beneficial solitude; the garden
of the Virgin and the garden of love which borrowed its
imagery; *sapientia* as well as *scientia* (good and bad
knowledge). Behind it all are the gardens of the Bible,
in Genesis, in the Song of Songs, in the New Testament
(Christ was *hortulanus,* a gardener). The perpetuation of
such complexities is a feature of seventeenth-century

poetry, and normally they are very difficult to discuss. Here, however, the issue is unusually clear. If one liked the art of gardening, or meant to praise it, one used the topics to this end. Thus William Harrison, in 1581, says that English gardening has come along very fast recently, as Pliny said it had at Rome:

> How art helpeth nature in the daily coloring, doubling and enlarging the proportion of our flowers, it is incredible to report: for so curious are our gardeners now in these days, that they presume to do in a manner what they list with nature. . . . It is a world also to see how many strange herbs, plants and annual fruits are daily brought unto us from the Indies, Americas, Taprobane [Ceylon], Canary Isles, and all parts of the world.

He does however pray that the British should use these benefits to the glory of God and not "unto further excess and vanity." To Harrison, the skill of gardeners is in no way deplorable: he says they "are not only excellent in graffing the natural fruits, but also in their artificial mixtures, whereby one tree bringeth forth sundry fruits, and one and the same fruit of divers colors and tastes, dallying as it were with nature and her course . . . of hard fruits they will make tender, of sour sweet, of sweet yet more delicate, bereaving also some of their kernels, others of their cores." Eighty years later, in Marvell's time, Evelyn says the same kind of thing in a more up-to-date way, though still remembering to counter the charges of luxury. The antithetical strain is constant; it recurs in gardening, philosophy, aesthetics, poetry, and, perhaps, corresponds to an habitual oscillation in our minds between freedom and enforcement, nature and custom. Marvell's originality, therefore, can only be the originality with which he states his antithesis and makes his thoughts brilliant.

Lascivious garden poetry was in vogue. Thomas Randolph, congratulating his moral friend Owen Felltham on his *Resolves,* calls that book a garden, meaning that it restores the one lost by Adam; but feigning a fear that this may be misinterpreted, adds:

> It is a garden; ha, I thus did say,
> And maids and matrons blushing run away.

Randolph, as it happens, is associated more closely with Marvell's poem. He wrote *Upon Love Fondly Refused for Conscience' Sake* in the measure of Horace's epode; he remembered Pliny's trick tree, and also the sexual connotations of grafting. Marvell took up the measure, used grafting as a figure for sexual procuring, meaning interference with plant sexuality for profit or art, and extended his condemnation to gardens in general. All this he put in the mouth of a mower.

Shakespeare has a masque of mowers, the critic Scaliger admits mower-eclogues as a class, and Remy Belleau has a stylised tapestry of mowers; they occur also in the poet Benlowes, whose work Marvell knew. But Marvell's mower is an original figure; perhaps Marvell chose a mower for this poem because he wanted a figure we should easily identify with unenclosed fields as against gardens (a more relevant figure than a shepherd like Spenser's Meliboee, who holds roughly the same attitude); and perhaps he then saw the chance to make brilliant the ordinary pastoral conceits by working them in terms of mower rather than shepherd. At any rate, only the mowers of *Upon Appleton House* share anything with Belleau and Benlowes, and the mower of the present poem is the voice of a naturalist thesis rather than the sophisticated Damon. Like the pleader in Papirius, he stands outside the great garden and condemns it as an emblem of luxury and decadence: nature enclosed, the flowers stupefied by over-feeding, or, growing double, symbols of duplicity; the natural color and scent of flowers altered by the meddling gardeners so much admired by Harrison and Evelyn. The flowers paint, though nature abhors makeup, *odit natura fucus*. The mower also deplores exotics. In Randolph's poem, the insertion of a graft into a "female" stock is an argument for love; for the mower, it is the corruption of natural sexuality. The gardener is a pandar, breaking not only the natural law but the Old Law of the Bible. The fruit is "uncertain and adulterate," like those peaches with almonds instead of stones celebrated by Evelyn, or the new flavors mentioned by Pliny and Harrison. The cherry grows on a "sterile" trunk; this, or more probably "without a stone" is the real sense of "without a sex." Nature is raped by art; as Papirius said, the people responsible prefer the imitation to the real, the statue before the true garden god.

The other Mower poems are at least proof of the poet's power, so highly valued and so valuable, to detect novelty in old situations. The novel pastoral hero enables the poet to produce a new elegant conceit on a theme as old as "all flesh is grass." *The Mower to the Glowworm*s has a witty delicacy superior to that of Lovelace's *Grasshopper,* and a wholly Marvellian ambience. *The Mower's Song* has the same strong and subtle grace in the expansion of a pastoral conceit, and even the slight clumsiness of the refrain is an adornment, miming the sweep of a scythe, which is in itself ungraceful.

THE GARDEN

Much of what is said about *The Mower against Gardens* will serve equally as an introduction to *The Garden*. Like the other poem, it is always confronting a silent set of antithetical attitudes, and from this it derives its wit. Like Adam, the poet is placed *in paradiso deliciarum,* in a paradise of delights, and like him he has a duty to contemplate their source. The resemblance to Adam, we are told, is rather to the man alone, to the period before Eve's creation; the poet echoes St. Ambrose's misogyny and Joseph Hall's: "I do not find that man, thus framed, found the want of a helper. His fruition of God gave him fullness of contentment." This situation does not require to be explained in the language of hermeticism or alchemy; there is no hermaphrodite, no conflict between sense and mind, no code. The points are made within the large context of garden topics sketched above. The poem makes the green of the garden stand for solitude against crowds, retirement against action, sensual delight free of sexual pursuit, the satisfaction of the senses against that of the mind; it is not the green of hope, the *benedicta viriditas* of alchemy, the green of the hermetic emerald, but the poem's green. Within its shade, the poet galls the horsemen of the opposition. Perhaps Marvell was again thinking of Randolph—the opening stanza of that poet's *Pastoral Courtship,* at any rate, introduces an antithetical garden, in which all trees combine to form, not the garland of repose but a bower for lovemaking:

> Behold these woods, and mark, my sweet,
> How all the bows together meet.
> The cedar his fair arms displays,
> And mixes branches with the bays.
> The lofty pine deigns to descend,
> And sturdy oaks do gently bend,
> One with another subtly weaves
> Into one loom the various leaves,
> As all ambitious were to be
> Mine and my Phyllis' canopy!

Marvell's tone is always light. The second stanza plays wittily on the plants as virtues, a theme familiar in Bible commentary, and on the old paradox that solitude is more pleasantly companiable than company. By the same token, it is more amorous than love, a paradox stated in terms of the emblematic colors of solitude and love. Ever since Ovid's Oenone pastoral lovers have cut the name of the desired person on trees; what we really should do, it seems to follow, is to cut on trees their own names. Gods chased girls not for sex but to turn them into trees. And so the paradoxes continue. The figures of natural abundance are as old as Hesiod; like Adam, the solitary has easily what others must labor for, and, unlike Adam, he may fall without being greatly upset. However, neither for him nor Adam is sensual repletion all; the garden provides more than a mirror of creation, since it also enables the mind to withdraw from sensibilia and produce its own fantasies, establishing worlds other than the visible. Thus begins a formal garden ecstasy; but there is still an element of antithesis carried over from the earlier wit: this ascending love is traditionally, in the familiar Platonic formula, contrasted with that which descends to mere sensual contact. The soul, ascended, is as it were between the worlds, like a bird on a bough; the figure was used by Spenser, also. It is poised between the white light of eternity and the varieties of color that light assumes in the creation. This, we learn, was the position of Adam before Eve and the Fall; there is a newly witty reprise of the earlier antitheses on love. After this exercise comes a quiet close, but it is still constructed as an antithesis. Other sundials boast that they count only sunny hours, depending on the unmediated light of direct sunshine; this one, which is a new kind of sundial (he is calling the garden a sundial), reckons hours much more sweet and wholesome; its light is filtered through the greenness of trees and so is "milder." Its face is not figures cut in stone, but flowers, which yield to us, as to the bee, sweetness and light.

I have made *The Garden* sound as simple as possible because the tone and content of few poems in the English language have been so misunderstood; the first ignored and the second fantasticated in a manner more pleasing to scholarly clumsiness than to poetic wit. It is a learned poem, in its way, but it has been packed with learned lumber; we have gained a heap of studious conjectures and almost lost a good poem.

UPON APPLETON HOUSE

To a lesser extent, this poem has been similarly mishandled. It is a most original work, but stands within a tradition of country-house poetry going back to Horace and Martial, with many seventeenth-century English, French and Italian examples. Even its conceited manner, the "semi-burlesque" and "Clevelandish description" of Leishman's terminology, is not unique, and corresponds to what Odette de Mourgues calls *précieux*.[1]

---

[1] Odette de Mourgues, *Metaphysical, Baroque and Précieux Poetry.* New York and London: Oxford University Press, 1953.

The English history of the genre is studied by G. R. Hibbard,[1] who associates it with a way of life that declined after 1660, so that Marvell's poem is about the last of the line. The old way of life was represented in the architecture, with the hall dominant, and stateliness sacrificed to function. Marvell makes a point of this in the opening stanzas, incidentally scoring off the French poet Saint-Amant as he does so. But if Appleton House reflects an orderly master and an orderly nature, the poet applies to them all a fantastic wit, institutes extraordinary comparisons, set-pieces such as the "catalogue of impossibilities" in the flood and mowing passages. Marvell's is much longer than other English examples, and, like his French contemporaries, he gets in many different things: praise of the patron's house (1–80); its history, with the attack on the nuns (81–280); the garden laid out in military style, the military figures merging with a lament for the devastation of civil war, etc. (281–368);[2] the mowing tableau (369–480); praise of the woods leading to an account of solitary study in the book of the creatures (481–624); the river (625–648); Maria Fairfax considered fantastically as the model and mistress of the natural scene (649–768); and a conceited conclusion.

The variety of all this defeats attempts to prove that the poem has real uniformity, whether ideological or rhetorical. Marvell is concerned with the play of a modern wit over what the French called a *tableau fantasque,* on finding local and novel uses for ancient themes such as the *adunata* ("catalogue of impossibilities") and for tran-

[1] *Journal of the Warburg & Courtauld Institutes,* xix (1956), 159–74. For the earlier history see Leishman, pp. 253ff., and Allen, pp. 119–26 (Selected Bibliography, p. xlv–xlvi).

[2] See Røstvig, p. 250, and Allen, pp. 132ff. (Selected Bibliography, p. xlv–xlvi). This seems overelaborate at times, for example in treating the two rails as allegorical, the first of Charles I and the second the live one, of Scotland (Fairfax disagreed with the execution of the King and the Scottish campaign of Cromwell). Miss Røstvig uses the resources of typology and hermeticism to establish moral and spiritual allegories also; the flood refers to the crossing of the Red Sea, with its typological meanings. According to Allen, Maria is Heavenly Wisdom, according to Røstvig, "the vapour of the power of God." Small allowance is made for the essential intermittency of the allegory.

sient allegories meant only to flicker through the mind; he even teases himself for finding them so readily ("Thus I, easy philisopher . . ."). The emblems and the occasional minute details belong to a fashionable poetry, that *"stravaganza della miope osservation"* found in baroque poetry by Croce.[1] One finds similar things in Cotton, or in Théophile de Viau; what is novel is the tone. There is nothing new about, for example, the story of fish living on land during a flood; it is told in the *Roman de la Rose.* Even the *types* of witty comment are old. But Marvell is never so raw as Cotton, nor so expansive as the French; he preserves the necessary qualities of surprise, pace, and variety without forfeiting detachment and delicacy; and beneath the jokes there is always the possibility of more serious allusion. At the slaughter of the rail, Thestylis makes first a joke about the poet calling the mowers Israelites, and speaking better than he knew; and then a joke about the Bible. Marvell moralizes unseriously on the dangers of the rail's nesting-place (if they avoid death by malice, they meet it by accident) and thinks up the comparison between the cries of the bereaved parents and muted trumpets. The hay looks like corpses on a battle-field, and "hay" is also a useful name for the victory dance; the mowers' sweat must smell sweet because they, like Alexander, have conquered the world. Underneath the wit, there are realms of serious reference, but you should glance over them; if you dwell too long, you lose the tone. Maria Fairfax is a meteorological freak, an unterrestrial meteor; she is also mistletoe on the trunk of her father. The poet in the wood is an inverted tree, and you may think of hermetic, Aristotelian, Platonic, or Rabelaisian references; but only briefly. There is no inherent solemnity. Parallels with Henry More will not survive a reading of *Psychozoia,* which is the kind of poem many critics seem to think Marvell was trying to write. But there is learning at the service of an athletic intelligence, the intelligence of the Horatian Ode.

1 *Storia della barrocca in Italia,* 1929, p. 257.

THE NYMPH COMPLAINING FOR THE DEATH OF HER FAWN

This is another poem which attracts the wrong kinds of solemnity. Is it uniformly allegorical? Is it "about" the history of the Church of England, or some other single topic? How is it to be related to the Song of Songs? Miss Wallerstein sensibly wrote that, like Solomon's Song, it lacked continuous or systematic allegory, but lent itself to shifting meanings in an allegorical field. Marvell thinks not only of the Song, but of Silvia's fawn, shot by Ascanius (*Aeneid,* vii, 475ff.—a pet she had tamed and bathed and combed; her lament started a war). Perhaps he remembered the hind in the *Punica* of Silius Italicus (xiii) whose wanton killing caused more fighting. Marvell treats these simple *casus belli* in the voice of the nymph herself, pastorally simple, saying more than she knows; he was aware of a long and rich tradition in which sophisticated poets write of the simple act of lamenting their pets, and the wit of the poem arises from this situation.

Before one considers the rival interpretations and decides which uniform allegory to vote for, he should study the tone of the *Complaint,* which is, of course, dramatic. Not only does the girl speak naïvely; her opinions and her range of reference are decorously limited, as is her understanding of the crafty gifts and puns of Silvio. It is a tone familiar from the Greek Anthology to the Pléiade; later, in an eclogue written into *Almahide* by Mme. de Scudéry, a lover presents a fawn in ninety-four stanzas, and the author says "I don't know if that bored you, but I have a great fondness for such woodland poetry (*poésie bocagère*) and that made me think you might not be displeased by its naïveté." Marvell is, as always, original; the naïveté is only the ground of his effects. Why, we ask, should the girl know about "deodands," which we have to look up? Our surprise suggests that we are listening to an intelligent child commenting on an adult situation; and we should remember that when we consider the tone of the whole poem. There are religious allusions; but the nymph is between us and the allusions. She has fewer points of reference than we; when

she says "There is not such another in / The world, to
offer for their sin," she does so because of her limited
experience and instruction; one innocent death recalls the
language and imagery of the archetypal sacrifice; the figure
is excessive, unless we revise it in obscure and complicated
ways, so that our complexity finally joins her simplicity.
The trick, as in simpler pastorals, is to please us by allow-
ing us to find reflections of our widely educated, grown-
up thoughts in the purer and simpler pastoral experience.

So the poem wavers between simplicities we can, as an
audience, pity (we could never ourselves be found in such
a situation) and simplicities in which our maturity is
invited to find charmingly rich and subtle implications.
Where else but in the Song of Songs would a nymph so
purely educated, so *bien élevée,* find language for her pet's
crisis? "My beloved is mine and I am his: he feedeth
among the lilies . . . turn, my beloved, and be thou like
a roe or a young hart . . . my beloved is gone down into
his garden, to the bed of spices, to feed in the gardens, and
to gather lilies . . . he feedeth among the lilies . . . I am the
rose of Sharon, and the lily of the valley." Behind her
words, for us (as the poet calculates) are the immense,
fluctuating, intermittent allegories which have accreted
round the Song of Songs. The beloved is Christ, and a
saint, which is what the nymph compares her fawn to,
is an imitator of Christ. The basis of the poet's calcula-
tion is the varying resonance of certain simple types of
language in controlled dramatic situations: there are
instances of this, where the exegetes can similarly spell
it all out too painstakingly, in *King Lear*.

Thus it is we, not the nymph, who are aware of certain
poignant contaminations, as when the relics are dedicated
to Diana, and the nymph is partly Niobe, partly the Virgin
at the foot of the Cross—a mixture, that is, of innocence
and presumption, like her own language. Certainly the
poem transcends its genre, the lament for a pet, and
certainly it glides over allegorical depths. The nymph
becomes a figure for the point of junction between simple
passions and that "inexhaustible and terrible nebula of
emotions" which attend them; and all our critical con-

fusions, our failure to hear the full range of tones, turn
on that point.

TO HIS COY MISTRESS. DIALOGUE BETWEEN THE RESOLVED SOUL AND CREATED PLEASURE. THE DEFINITION OF LOVE.

Readers of these poems need not be reminded that
Marvell did not invariably use his pastoral wit in love
lyrics and save magniloquence for politics. The lover in
To his Coy Mistress fights a Cromwellian war against
Time; he is active, restless, Machiavellian; he uses certain
ancient arguments against certain ancient rights. His
"philosophy" is hardly that of *The Garden,* or of the
Mower, though it is no less founded on a body of anti-
thetical topics. *Carpe diem* is older than Catullus. The
blason is old too—that catalogue of a girl's charms which
he sketches in derisive rejection, as implying false
doctrines of world and time. Her ancient rights presuppose
a whole world available to them in space (Ganges to
Humber) and filling the whole of time ("ten years before
the Flood" is near the beginning, "the conversion of the
Jews" heralds the Last Days). They can be dealt with
only in tones of strong masculine remonstration; when
they have been thoroughly discredited, he turns to the
real question of love in the world as it is, under the threat
of time; like Cromwell, he "urges his active star" and
prepares to "contract the scattered force of time."

What modernizes the old themes is intellectual power,
the attitude at once engaged and critical, the almost
physical energy. The ancient source of lines 25–32 is an
epigram of Asklepiades in the Greek Anthology (it has
many descendants): "You would keep your virginity?
What will it profit you? You will find no lover in Hades,
girl. It is among the living that we taste the joys of Kypris.
In Acheron, child, we shall only be bones and dust."[1]
"Virginity" always hovers between moral and physical
senses; Marvell firmly moves the stress to the physical.
"Honor" (protector of virginity or enemy of love) stands

---

[1] *Poems from the Greek Anthology,* translated by Forrest Reid. Lon-
don: Faber & Faber Ltd., 1943, p. 23.

in a similar position; and Marvell shifts the sense in much the same way, using it as fully synonymous with "hymen." Even "quaint" is used in this way; it is an old noun for the female sex organ. "Dust" and "ashes" remind us of The Order for the Burial of the Dead, but also tempt the mind to give "lust" a correspondingly physical sense for the man's body. The swirl of incomplete images (no time to work them out) in the final section is, I think, without parallel in the poetry of the period, but they retain their relation to *carpe diem*. No poem more strongly establishes Marvell as the poet of a civilization in change, of old forms in a new world, holding in the same thought justice and fate.

The *Dialogue between the Resolved Soul and Created Pleasure,* which Mary Palmer and her friends set at the head of *Miscellaneous Poems,* is altogether simpler, and was probably the libretto of a short cantata. Perhaps for this reason, it is the most undeviatingly schematic of all Marvell's poems. An understanding of the scheme would prevent certain unfruitful mistakes, like Legouis' shocked reaction to the "puritan" rejection of learning at the end. There is no space for full explanation here; sufficient to say that Marvell uses a prescribed scheme of temptations which was developed from Biblical commentary and poetry, and that he was content to illuminate it by conceits rather than radically change it.[1] It is, in a sense, a very simple model of his habitual procedures; the confusion of critics is also, unfortunately, characteristic, though they rarely have much to say about this strong and highly organized work.

The Definition of Love attracts more exegesis. Its title suggests that it belongs to the genre so named, but it is very unlike the other poems which belong to that genre (the most accessible is probably Ralegh's *Now what is Love*) and seems to resemble another kind of poem, which develops the topic "in love despair is nobler than hope." Stampa, a follower of Marino, has a poem called *Amante che si pregia di non avere alcuna speranza:* "a

---

[1] My article "The Banquet of Sense," *Bulletin of the John Rylands Library,* 44 (1961) 68–99, describes part of the background.

noble heart thinks its excellence diminished if hope
intrudes its flattering foot to reduce the ardent flames—
base comfort of common minds, depart! He who asks relief
values little his gentle torments." The *Chanson* in which
Desportes writes a somewhat similar argument also
represents the nobly hopeless love as splendidly contrary
to nature, and is that much closer to Marvell. In Marvell's
poem, all the dispositions of fate, including the structure
of the world, must be altered before the lovers may be
joined.

I see no need to follow Ann E. Berthoff's suggestion
(*Review of English Studies,* xii [1966], 18–29) that
Marvell is distinguishing between the love of a mistress
and the love of the exiled soul for heaven. As usual, the
depth and surprise of his variations make such interpreta-
tions possible; the temptation is to plot the remoter
harmonics and call them the tune. This overliteral inter-
pretation of irony and metaphor is very like the mis-
handling of allegory of which Rosemond Tuve complained
in her last book (*Allegorical Imagery,* Princeton, N. J.:
Princeton University Press, 1966, especially pp. 220ff.
and 409ff.).

To conclude: Marvell is not a philosophical poet; in
his role as poet he engaged his subjects as poetry, bringing
to them a mind of great intelligence and intelligently
ordered learning. Our knowledge of his religious and
political thought helps us only a little more than our
knowledge of his personal life (quick temper, preference
for solitary drinking) and can be related to the substance
of his poetry only very cautiously and generally (the
power of a mind engaged but detached, the alertness,
leaning on the wind). Negatively, we can learn a lot from
other poetry, and from the nature and contemporary use
of allegory (habitual intermittency defined by the cult of
acuteness or wit, and the resonantly defined detail). Broad
categories are misleading; using words such as "puritan,"
"Platonist," even such as "nature" and "wit," we must
constantly discriminate: wit is not seventeenth-century

property but an ancient instrument of poetry and of religion, nature an indescribably complex inheritance of assumptions and meanings. If *On a Drop of Dew* tempts you to call Marvell "Platonist," you are at once committed to centrifugal explanation, since it is "in logical conflict" with other poems, as Ruth Wallerstein saw (*Studies in Seventeenth-Century Poetic,* p. 232). You may then feel compelled to biography, stringing out the works in some order intended to display the changes and developments of Marvell's "thought." Miss Wallerstein was much nearer the mark when she said that Marvell "accepts elements of symbolic thought imaginatively without accepting them schematically" (p. 336), and we should extend this formula to include discursive thought also. Marvell seems to speak to our minds with an extraordinary directness and power, and the least we can do in return is to refrain from criticism which tends to reduce him to indirection and impotence. What everybody can agree on is that this poet has "wit and learning, with a singular penetration and strength of judgment."

FRANK KERMODE

Andrew Marvell

SELECTED POETRY

A General Note on the Text

The overall textual policy for the Signet Classic Poetry series attempts to strike a balance between the convenience and dependability of total modernization, on the one hand, and the authenticity of an established text on the other. Starting with the Restoration and Augustan poets, the General Editor has set up the following guidelines for the individual editors:

Modern American spelling will be used, although punctuation may be adjusted by the editor of each volume when he finds it advisable. In any case, syllabic final "ed" will be rendered with grave accent to distinguish it from the silent one, which is written out without apostrophe (e.g., "to gild refinèd gold," but "asked" rather than "ask'd"). Archaic words and forms are to be kept, naturally, whenever the meter or the sense may require it.

In the case of poets from earlier periods, the text is more clearly a matter of the individual editor's choice, and the type and degree of modernization has been left to his decision. But in any event, archaic typographical conventions ("i," "j," "u," "v," etc.) have all been normalized in the modern way.

JOHN HOLLANDER

A Note on this Edition

The principal authority for Marvell's poems is *Miscellaneous Poems. By Andrew Marvell, Esq; Late Member of the Honourable House of Commons, London, 1681*. This edition is referred to in the Notes as *1681*. Six poems included in that volume had been printed earlier. Two extant copies of 1681 have unusual importance: the first, in the British Museum, is the only known copy containing three poems which were canceled, presumably for political reasons, in *1681*, namely *An Horatian Ode upon Cromwell's Return from Ireland, The First Anniversary of the Government under O.C.*, and *A Poem upon the Death of O.C.* Of this last only lines 1–184 are in the B.M. copy. (Another copy, known to Margoliouth in 1920, contained the first and second parts of these poems, but has disappeared since.) The second important copy is one purchased by the Bodleian Library in 1945. In this, the three canceled poems have been added in a hand imitating print, and this volume is the authority for the text of *Upon the Death of O.C.* from line 185 to the end. The present text is based on these authorities but modernized. The arbitrary and frequent capitalizations of the original are reduced to lower case according to modern usage. Punctuation is also normalized. Variants are recorded in the notes only when they have some interest beyond the merely textual.

The textual situation grows much more difficult in Marvell's post-Restoration satires, which were generally circulated in many manuscripts before reaching print in the

series of *Poems of Affairs of State* (1689–1716). This
accounts for the difficulties that exist in determining which
of the satires are authentic and which are not. Scholarly
argument about the canon leaves Marvell with a dozen or
so satires (for a recent summing-up, see Legouis, pp.
163–64 and note 1) but some of these remain dubious,
and some are trivial; none, in my opinion, wins its place
in a selection of this length. Of the pre-Restoration poetry,
I have excluded all the Latin poems in *1681*, the poem
On the Victory of Blake over the Spaniards, and some
portions of the two long Cromwell poems. Enough is left,
I hope, to give an adequate impression of Marvell's pane-
gyric and satirical manners. The commendatory poem to
Lovelace's *Lucasta* was published in that book in 1649 and
not reprinted in *1681*. This is the only such poem I have
included. For the sake of completeness, I here mention
Upon the Death of Lord Hastings, published in a volume
of funeral elegies in 1649; and another funeral elegy, for
Lord Villiers, published separately in 1648 (?) and at-
tributed to Marvell by Margoliouth.

For obvious reasons, it is much easier to date the occa-
sional poems than the lyrics, and attempts to establish the
chronological order of these are hazardous and not very
useful. (Thus the *Dialogue between Thyrsis and Dorinda*
might be confidently placed in the early 1650s, with other
pastoral poetry of the "Nun Appleton period"; but we now
know that is was much earlier, probably of the late 1630s.)
I have therefore set out the contents of *1681* in order of the
original except that, following Margoliouth's sensible plan, I
have grouped together the satirical, commendatory and
political poems at the end and arranged them only in or-
der of composition.

Finally, a word about editions subsequent to *1681*, and
a few other relevant books. Thomas Cooke edited *The
Works* in two volumes (1726), but the most important
eighteenth-century edition is the three-volume *Works* of
Edward Thompson (1776) which contains the three
Cromwell poems. Grosart's four-volume edition of 1872
includes the prose works. In 1892 appeared Aitken's two-
volume Muses' Library edition of the poems. Margoli-

outh's Clarendon Press edition of *The Poems and Letters* in two volumes (1927, revised, 1952) superseded the others, though he does not print the prose. Hugh Macdonald did a new Muses' Library edition in one volume (1952). Also, there has been a great volume of comment on Marvell in recent years, with much bearing on interpretation and occasionally on the text.

Chronology

1621 March 31. Andrew Marvell born at Winestead-in-Holderness, Yorkshire, to the Reverend Andrew Marvell, the "facetious and yet Calvinistic" vicar of the town, and his wife, Anne Pease.

1624 Reverend Andrew Marvell appointed Lecturer in Holy Trinity Church, Hull.

1633 Andrew Marvell leaves Hull Grammar School, matriculates at Trinity College, Cambridge.

1637 Publishes first poem, *Ad Regem Carolum Parodia,* celebrating the birth of a fifth child to Charles I and imitating Horace's Actium Ode (*Carm.* i, 37) in a small volume which also includes poems by Crashaw and Edward King.

1638 Marvell's mother dies; his father remarries.

1639 Graduates B.A. Temporary conversion to Roman Catholicism. Father finds him in London and sends him back to Cambridge. (First Bishops' War.)

1640 (Second Bishops' War.)

1641 Marvell's father drowns. Excluded from Trinity (for neglect of duties?). (Long Parliament elected; it impeaches Strafford and Laud.)

1642 Civil War begins while Marvell is traveling abroad in Holland, France, Italy, and Spain. Before departure probably writes *Thyrsis and Dorinda,* perhaps other poems.

1643 (Abolition of episcopacy; death of Hampden; ordinance for licensing press.)

1644   (Parliamentary victory at Marston Moor; trial of
       Laud.)

1645   Marvell writes *Fleckno*. (Abolition of Prayer
       Book; execution of Laud; establishment of New
       Model Army; Parliamentary victory at Naseby.)

1646   (Presbyterian supremacy; King flies to Scotland.)

1647   (King seized, escapes to Isle of Wight; Army oc-
       cupies London.)

1648   Marvell writes commendatory poem for Lovelace's
       Lucasta (published 1649); possibly writes elegy
       on Francis Villiers, killed July 1648 in Royalist
       insurrection. (Second Civil War; Pride's Purge of
       Long Parliament.)

1649   Writes Hastings elegy. (Execution of King; proc-
       lamation of Commonwealth; Cromwell's Irish ex-
       pedition.)

1650   *An Horatian Ode* and *Tom May's Death*. (Crom-
       well's Scottish campaign.)

1651   Marvell tutor to Mary Fairfax at Fairfax's York-
       shire estates, including Nun Appleton. Publishes
       To His Worthy Friend Doctor Witty. (Coronation
       at Scone of Charles II; Battle of Worcester; flight
       of Charles II.)

1652   Marvell in Yorkshire. (Dutch War.)

1653   Receives Milton's recommendation for post of as-
       sistant Latin Secretary (Milton having become
       totally blind) but is not appointed; instead, be-
       comes tutor to William Dutton, Cromwell's future
       ward and prospective son-in-law; lives with Dut-
       ton in Oxenbridge's house at Eton. Writes *The
       Character of Holland* and perhaps *Bermudas*.
       (Cromwell expels Parliament; Protectorate estab-
       lished; defeat of Dutch.)

1654   December. Writes *The First Anniversary* (pub-
       lished 1655). (Parliament limits Cromwell's
       power.)

1655   (Foreign wars, rule of Major-Generals.)

1656   Marvell with Dutton in Saumur, France. A corre-
       spondent there calls him "a notable English Italo-

Machiavellian." (Toleration of Jews; end of rule of Major-Generals.)

1657 Writes poem celebrating Blake's victory over the Spaniards in the Canary Islands and the marriage songs for Mary Cromwell. Appointed Latin Secretary. (Cromwell declines crown.)

1658 *A Poem upon the Death of O.C.* (Cromwell dies, September 3; Richard Cromwell becomes Protector.)

1659 Elected Member of Parliament for Hull, a seat he holds for the rest of his life. (End of Protectorate.)

1660 Helps to save Milton during prosecution of regicides. (Charles II restored, enters London, May 29.) From this point I record fewer public events. However, Marvell's satires, not here included, represent a strong and consistently independent attitude to the royal family and government policy; henceforth he also made his name as a defender of religious and political tolerance.

1662 Exchanges blows with Thomas Clifford in the House. Spends ten months from May in Holland with Sir George Downing, the British Minister.

1663–65 Secretary to British embassies in Russia, Denmark, and Sweden.

1667 *Last Instructions to a Painter.* (Dutch fleet sailed up the Medway.) *Clarindon's House-Warming.* (Clarendon dismissed, August.)

1670 *The King's Vows* and Latin verses submitted in a competition for an inscription to be placed on a pediment of the French royal palace. (Secret Treaty of Dorn with French.)

1671 *Further Advice to a Painter* and *The Loyal Scot.* Marvell admires Blood's attempt to steal the crown jewels and may be associated with him in other enterprises.

1672 Approves the royal declaration of war against Holland, and the *Declaration of Indulgence.* Publishes *The Rehearsal Transpros'd,* Part I, against Samuel Parker, Archdeacon of Canterbury, and in favor of the King's policy of toleration of Jews. (Third Dutch War.)

1673 Parliament thwarts King on toleration, introducing Test Bill; Marvell writes *The Rehearsal Transpros'd,* Part II, to refute Parker again, rebut personal attacks on himself and his friends, and to plead for religious freedom. This book makes Marvell famous, and is a mainstay of his reputation in the succeeding century. His concern at the virtual certainty of the throne passing to the Catholic Duke of York causes him to turn away from Charles II. (Test Act compels resignation of Duke of York.)

1674 Commendatory verses on Milton's *Paradise Lost.*

1675 The "Statue" poems, parodying Charles II's speech from the throne, and *Mr. Smirke,* against the Anglican persecutors of Nonconformity (published 1676).

1676 Harbors his bankrupt Nonconformist kinsmen, the Thompson brothers, and Nelthorpe, in a house taken in the name of his housekeeper, Mary Palmer.

1677 Speaks in Commons against Bill to increase power of bishops; is forced to apologize to House for unseemly behavior to the Speaker. The King's secret dealings with the French provoke fears of Catholic plots, and Marvell writes *An Account of the Growth of Popery, and Arbitrary Government in England,* favoring toleration and control of monarchy by Parliament. (Marriage of William of Orange to Mary, daughter of Duke of York.)

1678 *Remarks upon a Late Disingenuous Discourse,* an attack on extremist Calvinist theology. Dies of an ague August 16. ("The Popish Plot.") Mary

1681 Palmer claims to be his widow as part of a plot to recover £500 he has deposited in his own name on behalf of the bankrupts Thompson and Nelthorpe. To lend credence to her imposture, she publishes the *Miscellaneous Poems* with a notice "To the Reader" which certifies that "all these Poems . . .

are Printed according to the exact Copies of my late
dear Husband, under his own Hand-Writing, being
found since his Death among his other Papers,
Witness my Hand this 15th day of *October,* 1680.
Mary Marvell."

Selected Bibliography

Editions of the Works:

The Poems and Letters of Andrew Marvell. 2 vols. H. M. Margoliouth (ed.). 2nd (revised) edition. New York: Oxford University Press, 1952. The standard edition.

The Poems of Andrew Marvell. Hugh Macdonald (ed.). (The Muses' Library). Cambridge, Mass.: Harvard University Press; London: Routledge & Kegan Paul, Ltd., 1952. Incorporates Bodleian MS. Eng. poet. d. 49; but the commentary is inferior and there are many slips.

Biographies:

Bradbrook, Muriel C. and M. G. Lloyd Thomas. *Andrew Marvell*. London: Cambridge University Press, 1940; Toronto: The Macmillan Co. of Canada, Ltd., 1941.

Legouis, Pierre. *André Marvell, poète, puritain, patriote*. New York and London: Oxford University Press, 1928. The most exhaustive study; the author summarizes much of it and brings it up to date in the next item.

————. *Andrew Marvell: Poet, Puritan, Patriot*. New York and London: Oxford University Press, 1965.

Criticism:

Allen, D. C. *Image and Meaning*. Baltimore: Johns Hopkins Press; London: Oxford University Press; Toronto: Burns & MacEachern, Ltd., 1960. Chapter 6 on *The Nymph Complaining* and Chapter 7 on *Upon Appleton House*.

Eliot, T. S. *Selected Essays*. New York: Daniel Ryerson, Inc.; London: Faber & Faber, Ltd., 1932, pp. 292–304. This, the best single essay on Marvell, and the inspiration of much later writing, has often been reprinted.

Hill, Christopher. *Puritanism and Revolution*. New York: Humanities Press, Inc.; London: Martin Secker & Warburg, Ltd.; Toronto: British Book Service (Canada), Limited, 1959. Chapter 13, "Society and Andrew Marvell."

Keast, William R. (ed.). *Seventeenth-Century English Poetry: Modern Essays in Criticism*. New York: Oxford University Press (Galaxy Books), 1962. Several well-known articles (by Frank Kermode, Leo Spitzer, Cleanth Brooks, and Douglas Bush) are collected in this volume.

Legouis, Pierre. "Marvell and the New Critics," *Review of English Studies,* new series, VIII (1957).

Leishman, James B. *The Art of Marvell's Poetry*. London: Hutchinson & Co., Ltd., 1966.

Poggioli, Renato. "The Pastoral of the Self," *Daedalus,* LXXXVIII (1959).

Røstvig, Maren-Sofie. *The Happy Man: Studies in the Metamorphoses of a Classical Ideal, 1600–1700*. Oslo: Akademisk Forlag, 1954; Oxford, Eng.: Basil Blackwell & Mott, Ltd., 1955.

Scoular, Kitty. *Natural Magic: Studies in the Presentation of Nature in English Poetry from Spenser to Marvell*. New York and London: Oxford University Press, 1965. Chapter 3, *Upon Appleton House*.

Stewart, Stanley. *The Enclosed Garden*. Madison, Wis.: University of Wisconsin Press, 1966.

Summers, J. H. "Marvell's Nature," *E. L. H.,* XX (1953).

Swardson, Harold R. *Poetry and the Fountain of Light*. Columbia, Mo.: University of Missouri Press; London: George Allen & Unwin, 1962, Chapter 4.

Toliver, Harold E. *Marvell's Ironic Vision*. New Haven: Yale University Press, 1965.

Wallerstein, Ruth. *Studies in Seventeenth-Century Poetic*. Madison, Wis.: University of Wisconsin Press, 1950.

The second part, entitled "The Various Light," is a long commentary on Marvell's poems.

Wedgwood, C. V. *Poetry and Politics under the Stuarts.* London: Cambridge University Press, 1960.

A DIALOGUE BETWEEN THE RESOLVED
SOUL AND CREATED PLEASURE°

Courage my Soul, now learn to wield
The weight of thine immortal shield.
Close on thy head thy helmet bright.
Balance thy sword° against the fight.
See where an army, strong as fair,　　　　　　5
With silken banners spreads the air.
Now, if thou be'st that thing divine,
In this day's combat let it shine:
And show that Nature wants an art
To conquer one resolvèd heart.　　　　　　10

Pleasure. Welcome the creation's guest,
Lord of earth, and Heaven's heir.
Lay aside that warlike crest,
And of Nature's banquet share:
Where the souls of fruits and flowers　　　　　15
Stand prepared to heighten yours.°

Soul. I sup above, and cannot stay
To bait° so long upon the way.

0 A Dialogue . . . Pleasure Probably intended for a musical setting,
though none has survived. For the design of the poem, see Introduc-
tion.　2–4 **shield . . . helmet . . . sword** Ephesians vi, 11, 13, 16, 17:
"Put on the whole armour of God, that ye may be able to stand
against the wiles of the devil. . . . Wherefore take unto you the whole
armour of God, that ye may be able to withstand in the evil day,
and having done all, to stand. . . . Above all, taking the shield of
faith. . . . And take the helmet of salvation, and the sword of the
Spirit, which is the word of God." The traditional equipment of
miles Christi.　15–16 **Where . . . yours** where the essences of fruits
and flowers will be ready to stimulate your (lower or sensitive) soul.
18 bait take food and drink during a pause in a journey.

Pleasure. On these downy pillows lie,
20   Whose soft plumes will thither fly;
              On these roses strowed so plain°
              Lest one leaf° thy side should strain.

Soul.   My gentler rest is on a thought,
              Conscious of doing what I ought.

25 *Pleasure.* If thou be'st with perfumes pleased,
              Such as oft the gods appeased,
              Thou in fragrant clouds shalt show
              Like another god below.

Soul.   A soul that knows not to presume
30   Is Heaven's and its own perfume.

Pleasure. Everything does seem to vie
              Which should first attract thine eye;
              But since none deserves that grace,
              In this crystal° view *thy* face.

35 *Soul.*   When the Creator's skill is prized,
              The rest is all but earth disguised.

Pleasure. Hark how music then prepares
              For thy stay these charming airs;
              When the posting winds recall,
40   And suspend the river's fall.

Soul.   Had I but any time to lose,
              On this I would it all dispose.
              Cease, Tempter. None can chain a mind
              Whom this sweet chordage° cannot bind.

---

21 **plain** flat. 22 **one leaf** referring to the legend of the Sybarite who claimed that his comfort was impaired by a single crumpled rose-petal. 34 **crystal** looking-glass. 44 **chordage** Behind the pun may be a recollection of St. Augustine who, in a famous passage on the senses, wrote that the pleasures of the ear had more firmly bound and subdued him than those of the lower senses (*voluptates aurium tenacius me implicaverant et subiugaverant*). William Empson calls the pun "exquisitely pointed especially in that most cords are weaker than *chains,* so that the statement is paradox, and these chords are impalpable, so that it is hyperbole." See the whole paragraph in the third chapter of *Seven Types of Ambiguity* (1930).

Chorus.   Earth cannot show so brave a sight   45
             As when a single soul does fence
             The batt'ries of alluring sense,
             And Heaven views it with delight.°
                    Then persevere, for still new charges
                       sound;
                    And if thou overcom'st thou shalt be
                       crowned.   50

Pleasure. All this fair, and soft,° and sweet,
                Which scatt'ringly doth shine,
             Shall within one beauty° meet,
                And she be only thine.

Soul.   If things of sight such heavens be,   55
             What Heav'ns are those we cannot see?

Pleasure. Wheresoe'er thy foot shall go
                The minted gold shall lie;
             Till thou purchase all below,
                And want new worlds to buy.   60

Soul.   Were't not a price who'd value gold?
             And that's worth nought that can be sold.

Pleasure. Wilt thou all the glory have
                That war or peace commend?
             Half the world shall be thy slave,   65
                The other half thy friend.

45–48 **Earth . . . delight** probably from Seneca's *Ecce spectaculum
dignum ad quod respiciat Deus . . . vir fortis cum mala fortuna
compositus* (L. N. Wall, *Notes & Queries*, 1961, pp. 185–86).
51 **soft** *1681* reads *coft;* Margoliouth's emendation is supported
by the discovery that in MS. Eng. poet. d.49 (Bodleian Library)—
a defective copy of *1681* with manuscript corrections—the same
emendation has been made, though it is not known by whom.
53 **within one beauty** The painter Zeuxis, believing that in nature
all possible beauties could not be found in one body (*uno in
corpore,* Cicero, *de Inventione,* ii) used many models for his
portrait of Helen. The theme was often moralized, e.g. by Petrarch,
Sonnets ii, 64, and by Ripa in the famous handbook *Iconologia*
(ed. of 1625, p. 610). Cowley has a similar passage in his poem
"The Soul."

Soul.   What friends, if to my self untrue?
               What slaves, unless I captive you?

Pleasure.   Thou shalt know each hidden cause,°
70   And see the future time;
                       Try what depth the center° draws,
                   And then to Heaven climb.

Soul.   None thither mounts by the degree°
               Of knowledge, but humility.°

75 *Chorus.*   *Triumph, triumph, victorious soul;*
               The world has not one pleasure more:°
               The rest does lie beyond the pole,
               And is thine everlasting store.

---

69 **cause** antecedent to natural phenomenon.   71 **center** the center
of the earth; point to which falling bodies tend, and so the lowest
point of the created world.   73 **degree** scale or ladder (with pun
on the academic sense).   74 **humility** of humility.   76 **not . . .**
more He has overcome all the temptations (Luke iv. 13).

ON A DROP OF DEW°

      See how the orient° dew,
    Shed from the bosom of the morn
      Into the blowing roses,
    Yet careless of its mansion new
    For° the clear region where 'twas born,   *5*
      Round in itself incloses,
    And in its little globe's extent,
Frames as° it can its native element.°
How it the purple flower does slight,
      Scarce touching where it lies,   *10*
    But gazing back upon the skies,
      Shines with a mournful light,
         Like its own tear,
Because so long divided from the sphere.
    Restless it rolls and unsecure,   *15*
      Trembling lest it grow impure,
Till the warm sun pity its pain,
And to the skies exhale it back again.
      So the soul, that drop, that ray

---

0 **On a Drop of Dew** Marvell also wrote a Latin version of this poem, entitled *Ros.* The poem has been criticized on the grounds that the comparison with manna enters too late, and forms a sort of appendix; but there is an old association between manna, dew and grace, and Marvell remembers it, probably, throughout his development of the analogue between the soul and the dew. 1 **orient** pearl-like. 5 **For** in favor of. 8 **as** so far as. 8 **native element** heaven (the sky).

20 Of the clear fountain of Eternal Day,
    Could it within the human flower be seen,
        Rememb'ring still° its former height,
        Shuns the sweet leaves and blossoms green;
        And, recollecting° its own light,
25 Does in its pure and circling thoughts express
    The greater heaven in an heaven less.
            In how coy a figure wound,
            Every way it turns away:
            So the world excluding round,°
30   Yet receiving in the Day.
            Dark beneath, but bright above,
            Here disdaining, there in love.
        How loose and easy hence to go,
        How girt° and ready to ascend;
35   Moving but on a point below,
            It all about does upward bend.
    Such did the manna's sacred dew distill;
    White, and entire, though congealed and chill.
    Congealed on earth; but does, dissolving,° run
40 Into the glories of th' Almighty Sun.

---

22 **still** always.   24 **recollecting** collecting again; remembering.
29 **So . . . round** thus shutting out the world round about it.
34 **girt** prepared for rapid movement.   39 **dissolving** See Exodus
xvi, 21.

THE CORONET

When for the thorns with which I long, too long,
    With many a piercing wound,
      My Savior's head have crowned,
I seek with garlands to redress that wrong:
    Through every garden, every mead,   *5*
I gather flowers (my fruits are only flowers),
    Dismantling all the fragrant towers°
That once adorned my shepherdess's head.
And now when I have summed up all my store,
    Thinking (so I myself deceive)   *10*
      So rich a chaplet° thence to weave
As never yet the King of Glory wore:
    Alas I find the Serpent old
    That, twining in° his speckled breast,
    About the flowers disguised does fold,   *15*
      With wreaths of fame and interest.
Ah, foolish man, that wouldst debase with them,
And mortal glory, Heaven's diadem!
But thou who only couldst the Serpent tame,
    Either his slipp'ry knots at once untie,   *20*
And disentangle all his winding snare;
Or shatter too with him my curious frame,°
And let these wither, so that he may die,
Though set with skill and chosen out with care:
That they, while thou on both their spoils dost tread,   *25*
May crown thy feet,° that could not crown thy head.

---

7 towers tall head-dresses.   **11 chaplet** coronet.   **14 twining in** entwining.   **22 curious frame** elaborately built structure.   **26 feet** When the serpent's head is bruised by Christ, he will, in the process, destroy the worthless poems offered him by the penitent; thus what could not serve to crown his head will, accidentally, crown his feet.

EYES AND TEARS°

How wisely Nature did decree,
With the same eyes to weep and see!
That, having viewed the object vain,
They might be ready to complain.

5   And, since the self-deluding sight,
In a false angle takes each height,°
These tears which better measure all,
Like wat'ry lines and plummets fall.

Two tears, which sorrow long did weigh
10   Within the scales of either eye,
And then paid out in equal poise,
Are the true price of all my joys.

What in the world most fair appears,
Yea even laughter, turns to tears:
15   And all the jewels which we prize,
Melt in° these pendants of the eyes.

I have through every garden been,
Amongst the red, the white, the green;

0 **Eyes and Tears** This conceited exercise is related to the vogue
for poems about tears, especially those of Mary Magdalen; Marvell
may have been thinking of Crashaw's *The Weeper*. See Leishman,
pp. 39ff.   5–6 **the . . . height** The sight, being liable to self-induced
error, makes wrong estimates of height by misjudging angles.
16 **Melt in** with the suggestion that they are inferior as jewels.

And yet, from all the flowers I saw,
No honey, but these tears could draw.   20

So the all-seeing sun each day
Distills the world with chemic ray;
But finds the essence only showers,
Which straight in pity back he pours.°

Yet happy they whom grief doth bless,   25
That weep the more, and see the less;
And, to preserve their sight more true,
Bathe still their eyes in their own dew.

So Magdalen, in tears more wise
Dissolved those captivating eyes,   30
Whose liquid chains could flowing meet
To fetter her Redeemer's feet.

Not full sails hasting loaden home,
Nor the chaste lady's pregnant womb,
Nor Cynthia teeming° shows so fair,   35
As two eyes swoln with weeping are.

The sparkling glance that shoots desire,
Drenched in these waves, does lose its° fire.
Yea, oft the Thund'rer pity takes
And here the hissing lightning slakes.   40

The incense was to Heaven dear,
Not as a perfume, but a tear.
And stars show lovely in the night,
But as they seem the tears of light.

21–24 **the . . . pours** The sun, like an alchemist, extracts each day
the essence of the world, but it turns out to be moisture, which
is then poured back. 35 **Cynthia teeming** Full moon. 38 **its** *it*
in *1681*, probably a misprint.

45 Ope then, mine eyes, your double sluice,
And practice so your noblest use.
For others too can see, or sleep;
But only human eyes can weep.

Now like two clouds dissolving, drop,
50 And at each tear in distance stop:
Now like two fountains trickle down:
Now like two floods o'erturn and drown.

Thus let your streams o'erflow your springs,
Till eyes and tears be the same things:
55 And each the other's difference bears;
These weeping eyes, those seeing tears.

BERMUDAS°

Where the remote Bermudas ride
In th' ocean's bosom unespied,
From a small boat, that rowed along,
The list'ning winds received this song.
    "What should we do but sing his praise   *5*
That led us through the wat'ry maze,
Unto an isle so long unknown,
And yet far kinder than our own?
Where he the huge sea-monsters° wracks,
That lift the deep upon their backs,   *10*
He lands us on a grassy stage,
Safe from the storms, and prelates' rage.
He gave us this eternal spring,
Which here enamels everything;

0 **Bermudas** John Oxenbridge, in whose house at Eton Marvell lived in 1653, had twice been to the Bermudas, first in 1635 as a result of the ecclesiastical persecutions. The islands, thus associated with Puritan exile, had for long been celebrated as a kind of earthly paradise, and the traditional attributes of that place associated with them. They were sometimes known as the Somers Islands, in memory of the captain whose wreck there gave rise to pamphlets on which Shakespeare drew in *The Tempest*. These already suggest that the islands were a paradise, with continual spring and summer together, rich in natural resources and reserved for the godly English. All the traditional lore of the earthly paradise became attached to the Indies, especially Bermuda; see, for instance, Ralegh's *History of the World*, pp. 21, 36; and H. R. Patch, *The Other World*, 1950, Lovejoy and Boas, *Primitivism and Related Ideas in Antiquity*, 1935, pp. 50ff. and J. W. Bennett, *S.P.* liii (1956) 114–140. Leishman, 277ff., adds something and discusses the well-known parallels with Waller's poem, *The Battle of the Summer Islands*, published in 1645. To summarize, the conventional description of the earthly paradise, with a few specific details added, had been very generally applied to the Bermudas from the time of John Smith's *Generall History of Virginia, the Somer Iles, and New England*, 1624, if not from that of the pamphlets used by Shakespeare.   9 **sea-monsters** Waller had written of a battle between Bermudans and stranded whales.

15 And sends the fowls° to us in care,
    On daily visits through the air.
    He hangs in shades the orange bright,
    Like golden lamps in a green night:°
    And does in the pomegranates close,
20 Jewels more rich than Ormus° shows.
    He makes the figs our mouths to meet,
    And throws the melons at our feet:
    But apples° plants of such a price,
    No tree could ever bear them twice.
25 With cedars,° chosen by his hand,
    From Lebanon, he stores the land:
    And makes the hollow seas, that roar,
    Proclaim° the ambergris° on shore.
    He cast (of which we rather boast)
30 The Gospel's pearl upon our coast:
    And in these rocks for us did frame
    A temple, where to sound his name.
    Oh let our voice his praise exalt,
    Till it arrive at heaven's vault:
35 Which thence (perhaps) rebounding, may
    Echo beyond the Mexique Bay.°"
          Thus sang they, in the English boat,
    An holy and a cheerful note,
    And all the way, to guide their chime,
40 With falling oars they kept the time.

---

15 **fowls** William Strachey, in his *True Repertory of the Wracke*, 1610, published in *Purchas his Pilgrimes*, 1625, describes at length how one easily caught a kind of bird something like a plover and "fat and full as a Partridge."   18 **golden . . . night** perhaps borrowed, as suggested by Maren-Sofie Røstvig, *The Happy Man*, 1954, p. 470, from Sherburne's

> . . . close-weaved branches a new Heaven present
> And to the sight form a green firmament:
> In which like fixed stars might espy
> Gold-colored apples glitter to the eye.

20 **Ormus** Hormuz, on the Persian Gulf.   23 **apples** pineapples. 25 **cedars** perhaps borrowed from Waller.   28 **proclaim** make manifest.   28 **ambergris** fragrant substance excreted by sperm whales. 36 **beyond . . . Bay** in order, presumably, to convert the heathen and the papist in South America.

CLORINDA AND DAMON°

C.   Damon, come drive thy flocks this way.
D.   No, 'tis too late; they went astray.
C.   I have a grassy scutcheon° spied,
     Where Flora blazons all her pride.
     The grass I aim to feast thy sheep;   *5*
     The flowers I for thy temples keep.
D.   Grass withers; and the flowers too fade.
C.   Seize the short joys then, ere they vade.°
     Seest thou that unfrequented cave?
D.   That den?
C.   Love's shrine.
D.   But virtue's grave.   *10*
C.   In whose cool bosom we may lie
     Safe from the sun.
D.   Not Heaven's eye.
C.   Near this, a fountain's liquid bell
     Tinkles within the concave shell.
D.   Might a soul bathe there and be clean,   *15*
     Or slake its drought?
C.   What is't you mean?
D.   These once had been enticing things,
     Clorinda, pastures, caves, and springs.

---

0 **Clorinda and Damon** For the pastoral dialogue, see notes on poem following.   3 **scutcheon** heraldic arms.   8 **vade** pass away, decay.

C.   And what late change?
D.   The other day
     Pan met me.
20 C.   What did great Pan° say?
D.   Words that transcend poor shepherds' skill,
     But he e'er since my songs does fill;
     And his name swells my slender oat.°
C.   Sweet must Pan sound in Damon's note.
25 D.   Clorinda's voice might make it sweet.
C.   Who would not in Pan's praises meet?

Chorus
Of Pan the flowery pastures sing,
Caves echo, and the fountains ring.
Sing then while he doth us inspire;
30   *For all the world is our Pan's choir.*

20 **Pan** Christ, as often in pastoral poetry.   23 **oat** flute.

A DIALOGUE BETWEEN THYRSIS
AND DORINDA°

Dorinda. When Death shall part us from these kids,
And shut up our divided lids,
Tell me, Thyrsis, prithee do,
Whither thou and I must go.

Thyrsis. To the Elysium.

Dorinda.   Oh where is't?   5

Thyrsis. A chaste soul can never miss't.

Dorinda. I know no way but one, our home;
Is our cell Elysium?

Thyrsis. Cast thine eye to yonder sky,
There the milky way doth lie;   10
'Tis a sure but rugged way,
That leads to everlasting day.

0 A Dialogue . . . Dorinda This pastoral dialogue—which resem-
bles many others written at the same period—seems to have been
one of Marvell's most popular poems. A version of it appears in
British Museum Additional MS. 31432, which is written in the
hand of the composer William Lawes, who was killed at the siege
of Chester in 1645. It seems therefore to be a very early poem, per-
haps belonging to the late '30s (Marvell being absent from England
in the early '40s), and it cultivates the same telicate *faux-naïf* we
find in one or two exquisite musical dialogues by Carew, Lovelace,
and Aurelian Townsend. Many such were set by Henry Lawes,
William's brother, who wrote the music for *Comus.* Marvell's poem
is also found in song books of 1659, 1663, and 1673. The sophisti-
cated modulation from erotic to religious imagery (admired by
T. S. Eliot in his tercentenary essay, where he speaks of *Clorinda
and Damon*) to some degree sets Marvell's pastoral dialogues apart
from the others.

Dorinda.   There birds may nest, but how can I,
                That have no wings and cannot fly?

15   *Thyrsis.*   Do not sigh, fair nymph, for fire
                Hath no wings, yet doth aspire
                Till it hit against the pole:
                Heav'n's the center° of the soul.

Dorinda.   But in Elysium how do they
20   Pass eternity away?

Thyrsis.   Oh, there's neither hope nor fear,
                There's no wolf, no fox, no bear;
                No need of dog to fetch our stray,
                Our Lightfoot we may give away;
25   No oat-pipe's needful, there thine ears
                May feast with music of the spheres.

Dorinda.   Oh sweet! oh sweet! How I my future state
                  By silent thinking, antedate:°
                I prithee let us spend our time to come
30   In talking of Elysium.

Thyrsis.   Then I'll go on: There, sheep are full
                Of sweetest grass, and softest wool;
                There, birds sing consorts,° garlands grow,
                Cool winds do whisper, springs do flow.
35   There, always is a rising sun,
                And day is ever but begun.°
                Shepherds there bear equal sway,°
                And every nymph's a queen of May.

Dorinda.   Ah me, ah me!
Thyrsis.   Dorinda, why dost cry?

---

18 **center** Compare *A Dialogue between the Resolved Soul and Created Pleasure*, line 71: there the center is that toward which physical objects tend, and the point here is that the soul has an exactly opposite center.   28 **antedate** anticipate.   33 **consorts** performances in harmony.   36 **day . . . begun.** It is always fresh morning.   37 **bear . . . sway** live in equality, without law (as usual in earthly and some other paradises).

Dorinda. I'm sick, I'm sick, and fain would die: 40
Convince me now that this is true;
By bidding, with me, all adieu.

Thyrsis. I cannot live without thee, I
Will for thee, much more with thee, die.

Chorus. Then let us give Carillo charge o' th' sheep,   45
And thou and I'll pick poppies and them steep
In wine, and drink on't even till we weep;
So shall we smoothly pass away in sleep.

A DIALOGUE BETWEEN THE SOUL AND BODY°

Soul.   O who shall from this dungeon raise
A soul enslaved so many ways?
With bolts of bones, that fettered stands
In feet; and manacled in hands:°
Here blinded with an eye; and there
Deaf with the drumming of an ear:
A soul hung up, as 'twere, in chains
Of nerves, and arteries, and veins;

0 **A Dialogue . . . Body** A note in the annotated Bodleian copy of *1681* suggests that this poem is incomplete; the second speech of the Body has four extra lines, which may have survived from a third rejoinder to the Soul. Debates between soul and body are not frequent in Renaissance poetry, and, indeed, occur, it appears, only in English. There are Anglo-Saxon and English thirteenth-century poems of this kind, but the revival of the form probably derives from medieval Latin examples. These develop the conflicts and paradoxes inherent in Galatians v. 17: "For the flesh lusteth against the spirit, and the spirit against the flesh: and these are contrary the one to the other." In a Latin poem surviving in a thirteenth-century manuscript in the library of Corpus Christi College, Cambridge, Caro (the Flesh) argues for sensual pleasure as natural and desirable, while Spiritus stresses the long and unpleasant consequences of this course. The fullest discussion of the medieval poems is in H. Walther, *Das Streitgedicht in den lateinischen Literatur des Mittelalters*, Munich 1920, especially p. 64 and pp. 215ff. See also F. J. E. Raby, *Secular Latin Poetry*, 1934, II, 299ff. Leishman, 210ff., gives several examples from English seventeenth-century poetry, none of them very closely resembling Marvell's strong paradoxical manner.   3–4 **bolts . . . hands** The violent antithesis between the function of the various organs from the points of view of soul and body is expressed by an assonance, an alliteration delayed and given point by the line-ending, and finally by an exploitation of the Latin root (*manus*—hand) of the verb, which represents hands as fetters. This prepares for the flatter paradox concerning the eye, and for the further paradox (reinforced by onamatopoeia) concerning the ear.

Tortured, besides each other part,
In a vain head, and double heart.°   *10*

Body.   O who shall me deliver whole,
From bonds of this tyrannic soul?
Which stretched upright, impales° me so,
That mine own precipice° I go;
And warms and moves this needless° frame   *15*
(A fever° could but do the same);
And, wanting where its spite to try,
Has made me live to let me die;
A body that could never rest,
Since this ill spirit it possessed.   *20*

Soul.   What magic° could me thus confine
Within another's grief to pine?
Where whatsoever it complain,
I feel, that cannot feel, the pain.°
And all my care itself employs,   *25*
That to preserve, which me destroys;°
Constrained not only to endure
Diseases, but, what's worse, the cure;

10 vain . . . heart So far, the organs have been literally treated,
as the physical agents of the soul's imprisonment. A characteristic
swerve of wit now uses *head* and *heart* ambiguously; they are still
parts of the anatomy of the soul's prison, but carry also the figura-
tive senses of egotism and treachery.   13 impales The Body is also
a prisoner, held erect and penetrated by the animal function of
the soul, given a life that is a mere preparation for death, and as if
possessed by a demon.   14 precipice "After he was stretch'd to such
an height in his own fancy, that he could not look down from top
to toe but his Eyes dazled at the Precipice of his Stature," Marvell,
Rehearsal Transpros'd, line 64, quoted by Margoliouth. Marvell en-
joyed the word; see *Upon Appleton House*, line 375.   15 needless un-
necessary.   16 A fever perhaps a reminiscence of Donne, *A Feaver*;
the disease stimulating the corrupt flow of animal spirits.   21 magic
referring to the common magical torment of enclosing familiar
spirits in trees.   23–24 whatsoever . . . pain "It" is the body.
Whatever *it* suffers, *I* experience the pain of, although (except in-
sofar as I animate a body) I am immaterial and so impervious to
pain.   25–26 all . . . destroys I am obliged to devote myself to the
preservation of a body whose health is directly opposed to my
interests.

And ready oft the port° to gain,
30   Am shipwrecked° into health again.

Body.   But physic yet could never reach
The maladies° thou me dost teach:
Whom first the cramp of hope does tear;
And then the palsy shakes of fear:
35   The pestilence of love does heat;
Or hatred's hidden ulcer eat:
Joy's cheerful madness does perplex,
Or sorrow's other madness vex:
Which knowledge forces me to know,
40   And memory will not forgo.
What but a soul could have the wit
To build me up for sin so fit?
So architects do square and hew,
Green trees that in the forest grew.°

29 **the port** death.   30 **shipwrecked** The paradox of the happy
shipwreck is employed in Shakespeare's *The Tempest* and its
sources; also by Crashaw in a Latin epigram *Ad Bethesdae piscinam
naufragium* which Marvell probably knew. There is a French
seventeenth-century ballet called *Ballet du naufrage beureux* by
Claude de l'Estoille (on whom see A. Adam, *Histoire de la littéra-
ture française au XVIⁱᵉ siècle*, I [1948] p. 361).   32 **maladies** Here
spiritual ills are rendered in physical terms, as befits the body.
43–44 **So . . . grew** The emphasis is on the perversity of the soul
in altering what was natural (indifferent to sin) into something
which could, like a building, be occupied by it. Marvell is re-
membering a story told by Plutarch (*Moralia* 210e) about Agesilaus,
who noticed that in Asia squared timber was used for building.
He asked if the trees grew square in those parts, and when they
said, "No, round," he retorted, "Would you make them round if
they grew square?" (Pointed out to me by Professor J. C. Maxwell.)

THE NYMPH COMPLAINING FOR THE
DEATH OF HER FAWN°

The wanton troopers° riding by
Have shot my fawn and it will die.
Ungentle men! They cannot thrive
To kill thee. Thou ne'er didst alive
Them any harm: alas, nor could   5
Thy death yet do them any good.
I'm sure I never wished them ill;
Nor do I for all this; nor will:
But, if my simple prayers may yet
Prevail with Heaven to forget   10
Thy murder, I will join my tears
Rather than fail. But, O my fears!
It cannot die so.° Heaven's King
Keeps register of everything:
And nothing may we use in vain.   15
Ev'n beasts must be with justice slain,
Else men are made their deodands.°
Though they should wash their guilty hands
In this warm life-blood, which doth part
From thine, and wound me to the heart,   20
Yet could they not be clean: their stain
Is dyed in such a purple grain.

0 **The Nymph . . . Fawn** Concerning antecedents, analogues and
interpretation, see Introduction. 1 **troopers** The word came into
use about 1640 and was applied to the invading army of the Cove-
nanters. 13 **so** forgotten, unavenged by Heaven. 17 **deodands**
Any chattel that caused the death of a man was forfeit under law
to the lord of the manor; the Nymph is saying that if men do not
kill beasts with justice, this rule ought to apply equally to them.
They would thus be deodands.

There is not such another in
The world, to offer for their sin.
25   Unconstant Sylvio, when yet
I had not found him counterfeit,
One morning (I remember well)
Tied in this silver chain and bell,
Gave it to me: nay, and I know
30 What he said then; I'm sure I do.
Said he, "Look how your huntsman here
Hath taught a fawn to hunt his *dear*."°
But Sylvio soon had me beguiled.
This waxèd tame, while he grew wild,
35 And quite regardless of my smart,
Left me his fawn, but took his heart.°
      Thenceforth I set myself to play
My solitary time away
With this; and very well content,
40 Could so mine idle life have spent;
For it was full of sport, and light
Of foot, and heart; and did invite
Me to its game; it seemed to bless
Itself in me. How could I less
45 Than love it? O I cannot be
Unkind, t' a beast that loveth me.
      Had it lived long, I do not know
Whether it too might have done so
As Sylvio did: his gifts might be
50 Perhaps as false or more than he.
But I am sure, for ought that I
Could in so short a time espy,
Thy love was far more better then°
The love of false and cruel men.
55   With sweetest milk, and sugar, first
I it at mine own fingers nurst:
And as it grew, so every day
It waxed more white and sweet than they.

32–36 **dear . . . heart** these very old pastoral puns are here used
as a contribution to the sophisticated naïveté of the tone.   53 **then**
than.

It had so sweet a breath! And oft
I blushed to see its foot more soft,   60
And white (shall I say than my hand?)
Nay, any lady's of the land.
   It is a wond'rous thing, how fleet
'Twas on those little silver feet.
With what a pretty skipping grace,   65
It oft would challenge me the race;
And when 't had left me far away,
'Twould stay, and run again, and stay.
For it was nimbler much than hinds;
And trod, as on the foùr° winds.   70
   I have a garden of my own,
But so with roses overgrown,
And lilies, that you would it guess
To be a little wilderness.
And all the spring time of the year   75
It only lovèd to be there.
Among the beds of lilies, I
Have sought it oft, where it should lie;
Yet could not, till itself would rise,
Find it, although before mine eyes: 80
For, in the flaxen lilies' shade,
It like a bank of lilies laid.
Upon the roses it would feed,
Until its lips ev'n seemed to bleed;
And then to me 'twould boldly trip,   85
And print those roses on my lip.
But all its chief delight was still
On roses thus itself to fill,
And its pure virgin limbs to fold
In whitest sheets of lilies cold.   90
Had it lived long, it would have been
Lilies without, roses within.
   O help! O help! I see it faint,
And die as calmly as a saint.
See how it weeps. The tears do come   95
Sad, slowly dropping like a gum.

---

70 foùr (disyllable).

So weeps the wounded balsam,° so
The holy frankincense doth flow.
The brotherless Heliades°
100 Melt in such amber tears as these.
        I in a golden vial will
Keep these two crystal tears; and fill
It till it do o'erflow with mine;
Then place it in Diana's shrine.
105   Now my sweet fawn is vanished to
Whither the swans and turtles go:
In fair Elysium to endure,
With milk-white lambs, and ermines pure.
O do not run too fast, for I
110 Will but bespeak thy grave, and die.
        First my unhappy statue shall
Be cut in marble; and withal,
Let it be weeping too—but there
Th' engraver sure his art may spare,
115 For I so truly thee bemoan,
That I shall weep though I be stone:°
Until my tears, still dropping, wear
My breast, themselves engraving there.
There at my feet shalt thou be laid,
120 Of purest alabaster made;
For I would have thine image be
White as I can, though not as thee.

97 **balsam** applied both to the balsam-tree and its resin.   99 **Heliades**
the three daughters of Helios, sisters of Phaeton, who, after mourn-
ing their brother's death, were transformed into amber-dropping
trees.   116 **stone** The nymph imagines her fate as parallel to that
of Niobe who, lamenting the death of all her children, was turned
to stone.

YOUNG LOVE

Come little infant, love me now,
   While thine unsuspected years
Clear thine agèd father's brow
   From cold jealousy and fears.

Pretty surely 'twere to see   *5*
   By young love old time beguiled:
While our sportings are as free
   As the nurse's with the child.

Common beauties stay fifteen;
   Such as yours should swifter move;   *10*
Whose fair blossoms are too green°
   Yet for lust, but not for love.

Love as much the snowy lamb
   Or the wanton kid does prize,
As the lusty bull or ram,   *15*
   For his morning sacrifice.

Now then love me; time may take
   Thee before thy time away:
Of this need we'll virtue make,
   And learn love before we may.   *20*

So we win of° doubtful fate;
   And, if good she to us meant,
We that good shall antedate;°
   Or, if ill, that ill prevent.

---

11 **green** immature.　21 **of** over.　23 **antedate** anticipate; cf. *Thyrsis and Dorinda*, line 28.

25 Thus as kingdoms, frustrating
        Other titles to their crown,
    In the cradle crown their king,
        So all foreign claims to drown;

    So, to make all rivals vain,
30   Now I crown thee with my love:
    Crown me with thy love again,
        And we both shall monarchs prove.

TO HIS COY MISTRESS°

Had we but world enough, and time,
This coyness, Lady, were no crime.
We would sit down, and think which way
To walk, and pass our long love's day.
Thou by the Indian Ganges' side   5
Should'st rubies find: I by the tide
Of Humber would complain. I would
Love you ten years before the Flood:
And you should, if you please, refuse
Till the Conversion of the Jews.°   10
My vegetable° love should grow
Vaster than empires, and more slow.
An hundred years should go to praise
Thine eyes, and on thy forehead gaze;
Two hundred to adore each breast;   15
But thirty thousand to the rest:
An age at least to every part,
And the last age should show your heart.°

---

0 **To his Coy Mistress** This poem is discussed in the Introduction.
10 **Conversion of the Jews** This will happen during the Last Days.
Attempts have been made to give this line a topical reference, but
it simply means "till almost the end of time." 11 **vegetable** grow-
ing as slowly as vegetation. 13–18 **An hundred . . . heart** The
hyperbole derives from the old *blason*, or catalogue of a mistress's
beauties, and is anticipated by Cowley in "My Diet" (*The Mistress*).

> On a sigh of pity I a year can live.
> One tear will keep me twenty at least.
> Fifty a gentle look will give,
> An hundred years on one kind word I'll feast;
> A thousand more will added be
> If you an inclination have for me;
> And all beyond is vast eternity.

For, Lady, you deserve this state;
20 Nor would I love at lower rate.
    But at my back I always hear
Time's wingèd chariot° hurrying near;
And yonder all before us lie
Deserts of vast eternity.
25 Thy beauty shall no more be found,
Nor, in thy marble vault, shall sound
My echoing song; then worms shall try
That long preserved virginity:
And your quaint honor° turn to dust,°
30 And into ashes all my lust.
The grave's a fine and private place,
But none I think do there embrace.
    Now therefore, while the youthful hue
Sits on thy skin like morning dew,°
35 And while thy willing soul transpires
At every pore with instant fires,°
Now let us sport us while we may;
And now, like am'rous birds of prey,
Rather at once our time devour,
40 Than languish in his slow-chapt power.°

22 **Time's . . . chariot** Time is often represented as winged, and often has a chariot; but the conflation appears to be Marvell's own. 29 **quaint honor** While this is perfectly intelligible as a figurative expression, abstract for concrete, Marvell is punning on other than the more common senses of the words, each of which is, in the English of the time, used concretely to mean the female pudenda. 29 **dust** *durst in 1681.* 34 **dew** *1681* reads *glew;* the present reading, Cooke's, is generally accepted, though Margoliouth in his first edition read *lew* ("warmth"), arguing that the printer repeated the last letter of "morning." This attractive conjecture he later abandoned, probably correctly, in favor of Cooke's. 35-36 **willing . . . fires** Despite her professed coyness, her amorous spirit shows in her flushed face; it breathes through every pore. Donne uses the same idea in a different context when he says of Elizabeth Drury that "her pure and eloquent blood/ Spoke in her cheeks" (*The Second Anniversary,* ll. 244-45). 40 **slow-chapt power** power of his slowly devouring jaws.

Let us roll all our strength, and all
Our sweetness, up into one ball,
And tear our pleasures with rough strife,
Thorough° the iron gates of life.
Thus, though we cannot make our sun   45
Stand still, yet we will make him run.°

41–46 **Let . . . run** There has been much discussion of the significance of these images. They are certainly discontinuous, and perhaps derive urgency from that. Margoliouth thinks that in line 42 Marvell is thinking of a pomander, and in line 44, "where the sexual strife is waged" the "gates of life" suggest the narrow reach known as the Iron Gate, which separates the upper from the lower Danube. Whether or not this is true, the line certainly refers to the act of defloration. The final couplet, as Christopher Hill first suggested (*Puritanism and Revolution*, 1958, p. 347, n. 1.), recommends that the lovers should not imitate Joshua's sun, which stood still, but David's, which came forth like a bridegroom to run his race. Cf. *The First Anniversary of the Government under O.C.*, lines 7–8:

> *Cromwell* alone with greater vigor runs
> (Sun-like) the stages of succeeding suns. . . .

Cromwell resembles the lover in other ways: he could "ruin the great work of Time" (*Horatian Ode*, l. 34) and it is also he who "the force of scattered time contracts,/ And in one year the work of ages acts" (*The First Anniversary*, ll. 13–14). **44 Thorough** through.

THE UNFORTUNATE LOVER°

Alas, how pleasant are their days
With whom the infant Love yet plays!
Sorted by pairs, they still are seen
By fountains cool, and shadows green.
5 But soon these flames do lose their light,
Like meteors of a summer's night:
Nor can they to that region climb,
To make impression upon time.°

'Twas in a shipwreck,° when the seas
10 Ruled, and the winds did what they please,
That my poor lover floating lay,
And, ere brought forth, was cast away;
Till at the last the master-wave
Upon the rock his mother drave;

0 **The Unfortunate Lover** This is one of the most extravagantly conceited, Clevelandesque, of Marvell's lyrics. Leishman finds in it a remarkable instance of the sixteenth- and seventeenth-century "emblematisation of metaphor, this way in which a poet compels his reader to visualise all the detail of a metaphor or simile or personification, instead of giving, as it were, more general directives to his imagination and allowing him to supply or withhold detail as he pleases" (p. 35). M. C. Bradbrook and Lloyd Thomas (*Andrew Marvell*, 1940, p. 29n.) relate the poem to a series of emblems depicting a lover's suffering in Otto van Veen's *Amorum Emblemata* (Antwerp, 1608). L. N. Wall suggests indebtedness to Lovelace's *Against the Love of Great Ones* (*Notes and Queries*, ccii, 170ff.).   6–8 **meteors . . . time** Meteors were thought to be exhalations of vapor from the interior of the earth; they ascended to the sphere of fire and burned out. If they could pass the sphere of fire and the moon they would reach a region of incorruptibility and timelessness.   9 **shipwreck** The lover's birth, by Cesarian section, is represented as a shipwreck.

And there she split against the stone,   15
In a Caesarean sectiòn.°

The sea him lent these bitter tears°
Which at his eyes he always bears:
And from the winds° the sighs he bore,
Which through his surging breast do roar.   20
No day he saw but that which breaks,
Through frightèd clouds in forkèd streaks;
While round the rattling thunder hurled,
As at the fun'ral of the world.

While Nature to his birth presents   25
This masque° of quarreling elements,
A num'rous fleet of corm'rants black,
That sailed insulting o'er the wrack,
Received into their cruel care
Th' unfortunate and abject heir: 30
Guardians most fit to entertain
The orphan of the hurricane.

They fed him up with hopes and air,
Which soon digested to despair:
And as one corm'rant fed him, still   35
Another on his heart did bill.°
Thus while they famish him, and feast,
He both consumèd, and increased;
And languishèd with doubtful breath,
Th' amphibium° of life and death.   40

And now, when angry heaven would
Behold a spectacle of blood,
Fortune and he are called to play
At sharp° before it all the day;
And tyrant Love his breast does ply   45

---

16 **section** (three syllables).   17–19 **tears . . . winds** The attributes of
the Petrarchan lover are explained here by the circumstances of his
birth.   26 **masque** show, representation.   36 **bill** peck.   40 **amphibium** a being that lives equally well in water and on land.   44 **at sharp** with unbated or sharpened weapons.

With all his winged artillery:
Whilst he, betwixt the flames and waves,
Like Ajax,° the mad tempest braves.

See how he nak'd and fierce does stand,
50   Cuffing the thunder with one hand;
While with the other he does lock,
And grapple, with the stubborn rock,
From which he with each wave rebounds,
Torn into flames, and ragg'd with wounds.
55   And all he says, a lover dressed
In his own blood does relish best.

This is the only banneret°
That ever Love created yet:
Who though, by the malignant stars,
60   Forced to live in storms and wars;
Yet dying leaves a perfume here,
And music within every ear;
And he in story only rules,
In a field sable a lover gules.°

48 **Ajax** referring to the hero's extravagant behavior when he went
mad with disappointment at not receiving the arms of the dead
Achilles.   57 **banneret** one created knight on the battlefield. Prob-
ably from Lovelace, *Dialogue—Lucasta, Alexis*, in *Lucasta*, 1649 (to
which Marvell contributed commendatory verses): "Love ne'er his
standard when his host he sets, / Creates alone fresh-bleeding ban-
nerets."   64 **In . . . gules** Heraldic terms—a red lover in a black field.

THE GALLERY°

Clora, come view my soul, and tell
Whether I have contrived it well.
Now all its several lodgings lie
Composed into one gallery;
And the great arras-hangings, made   5
Of various faces, by are laid;
That, for all furniture, you'll find
Only your picture in my mind.°

Here thou art painted in the dress
Of an inhuman murderess;   10
Examining° upon our hearts
Thy fertile shop° of cruel arts:
Engines° more keen than ever yet
Adornèd tyrant's cabinet;
Of which the most tormenting are   15
Black eyes, red lips, and curlèd hair.

But, on the other side, thou'rt drawn
Like to Aurora in the dawn;
When in the east she slumb'ring lies,
And stretches out her milky thighs;   20

---

0 **The Gallery Poems** describing real or imaginary galleries occur
among Marino and his followers, Italian and French, but I have
not met one that uses the topic in the same way as Marvell. L. N.
Wall (*Notes and Queries* ccii, 170ff.) suggests a debt to Lovelace's
Amyntor's Grove.   7–8 **for . . . mind** You will find that the mental
gallery contains only my pictures of you (the other "furniture" hav-
ing been put away).   11 **Examining** testing.   12 **shop** business
equipment (not in O.E.D.).   13 **Engines** instruments (of torture).

While all the morning choir does sing,
And manna falls, and roses spring;
And, at thy feet, the wooing doves
Sit perfecting their harmless loves.

25 Like an enchantress here thou show'st,
Vexing thy restless lover's ghost;
And, by a light obscure, dost rave
Over his entrails, in the cave;
Divining thence, with horrid care,
30 How long thou shalt continue fair;
And (when informed) them throw'st away,
To be the greedy vulture's prey.

But, against that, thou sit'st afloat
Like Venus in her pearly boat.
35 The halcyons,° calming all that's nigh,
Betwixt the air and water fly:
Or, if some rolling wave appears,
A mass of ambergris° it bears:
Nor blows more wind than what may well
40 Convoy the perfume to the smell.

These pictures and a thousand more,
Of thee, my gallery do store;
In all the forms thou canst invent
Either to please me, or torment:
45 For thou alone to people me,
Art grown a num'rous colony;
And a collection choicer far
Than or Whitehall's, or Mantua's were.°

---

35 **halcyons** These birds were thought to nest on the surface of the
sea and were thus regarded as ensuring calm at the nesting season.
38 **ambergris** See *Bermudas*, line 28.   48 **Whitehall's . . . were**
Charles I had made a great collection of paintings, partly by pur-
chasing those of Vincenzo Gonzaga, Duke of Mantua. This collec-
tion was ordered to be sold after the King's death by an Act of
Parliament (1650). It is argued that Marvell must have written the
poem or altered this and the preceding line after 1650. But "were"
may be subjunctive; and in any case the alteration ("are" to "were")
is an easy one.

But, of these pictures and the rest,
That at the entrance likes me best;   50
Where the same posture, and the look
Remains, with which I first was took:
A tender shepherdess, whose hair
Hangs loosely playing in the air,
Transplanting flowers from the green hill,   55
To crown her head, and bosom fill.

THE FAIR SINGER°

To make a final conquest of all me,
Love did compose so sweet an enemy,
In whom both beauties to my death agree,
Joining themselves in fatal harmony;
That while she with her eyes my heart does bind,
She with her voice might captivate my mind.

I could have fled from one but singly fair:
My disentangled soul itself might save,
Breaking the curlèd trammels of her hair.
But how should I avoid to be her slave,
Whose subtle art invisibly can wreathe
My fetters of the very air I breathe?

It had been easy fighting in some plain,
Where victory might hang in equal choice,
Who has th' advantage both of eyes and voice,
But all resistance against her is vain,
And all my forces needs must be undone,
She having gainèd both the wind and sun.

5 — That while she with her eyes my heart does bind,

10 — But how should I avoid to be her slave,

15 — But all resistance against her is vain,

0 **The Fair Singer** A common theme of the period, occurring in
Gongora, the Marinisti, the French poet Voiture (*Sur une belle
voix*), and in Carew, Lovelace, Cowley, Stanley, Waller, and Milton.

MOURNING

You, that decipher out the fate
Of human offsprings from the skies,
What mean these infants° which of late
Spring from the stars of Chlora's eyes?

Her eyes confused, and doubled o'er,   5
With tears suspended ere they flow,
Seem bending upwards, to restore
To heaven, whence it came, their woe:

When, molding off° the wat'ry spheres,
Slow drops untie themselves away;   10
As if she, with those precious tears,
Would strow the ground where Strephon lay.

Yet some affirm, pretending art,
Her eyes have so her bosom drowned,
Only to soften near her heart   15
A place to fix another wound.

And, while vain pomp does her restrain
Within her solitary bower,
She courts herself in am'rous rain;
Herself both Danaë° and the shower.   20

---

3 **infants** tears; but some editors think "babies" in the common
sense of the image of the lover as reflected in his mistress' eyes.
9 **molding off** (*molding of* in *1681*) forming themselves into a shape
which detaches itself from the eyes. But perhaps Marvell wrote
"molting." 20 **Danaë** She was visted by Jupiter in a shower of gold.

Nay others, bolder, hence esteem
Joy now so much her master grown,
That whatsoever does but seem
Like grief, is from her windows thrown.

25 Nor that she pays, while she survives,
To her dead love this tribute due;
But casts abroad these donatives,
At the installing of a new.

How wide° they dream! The Indian slaves
30 That sink for pearl through seas profound
Would find her tears yet deeper waves
And not of one the bottom sound.

I yet my silent judgment keep,
Disputing not what they believe;
35 But sure as oft as women weep,
It is to be supposed they grieve.

29 **wide** inaccurately.

DAPHNIS AND CHLOË°

Daphnis must from Chloë part;
Now is come the dismal hour
That must all his hopes devour,
All his labor, all his art.

Nature, her own sex's foe,   5
Long had taught her to be coy;
But she neither knew t' enjoy,
Nor yet let her lover go.

But, with this sad news surprised,
Soon she let that niceness fall;   10
And would gladly yield to all,
So it had his stay comprised.°

Nature so herself does use°
To lay by her wonted state,
Lest the world should separate;   15
Sudden parting closer glues.

0 **Daphnis and Chloë** This poem seems to be related to some lines
from Suckling's play *Aglaura* (III.i) where Aglaura asks Thersames
not to consummate their marriage at a critical moment in his life:

> Gather not roses in a wet and frowning hour,
> They'll lose their sweets then, trust me they will, sir,
> What pleasure can love take to play his game out,
> When death must keep the stakes?

(Mrs. E. E. Duncan-Jones, reported in Leishman, p. 121.) The
title, of course, is that of the pastoral romance of Longus. The
stanza, as Leishman points out, is that of Shakespeare's *The Phoenix
and Turtle*, and of Carew's *Separation of Lovers*. 12 **comprised**
included as a condition. 13 **does use** is accustomed.

He, well read in all the ways
By which men their siege maintain,
Knew not that the fort to gain
20 Better 'twas the siege to raise.

But he came so full possessed
With the grief of parting thence,
That he had not so much sense
As to see he might be blessed:

25 Till love in her language breathed
Words she never spake before;
But, than legacies no more,°
To a dying man bequeathed.

For, alas, the time was spent,
30 Now the latest minute's run
When poor Daphnis is undone,
Between joy and sorrow rent.

At that "Why?" that "Stay my dear,"
His disordered locks he tare;
35 And with rolling eyes did glare,
And his cruel fate forswear.

As the soul of one scarce dead,
With the shrieks of friends aghast,
Looks distracted back in haste,
40 And then straight again is fled;

So did wretched Daphnis look,
Frighting her he lovèd most.
At the last, this lover's ghost
Thus his leave resolvèd took:

45 "Are my hell and heaven joined
More to torture him that dies?
Could departure not suffice,
But that you must then grow kind?

"Ah my Chloë, how have I
50 Such a wretched minute found,

27 But . . . more But at this point they were mere legacies.

When thy favors should me wound
More than all thy cruelty?

"So to the condemnèd wight
The delicious cup we fill;
And allow him all he will   55
For his last and short delight.

"But I will not now begin
Such a debt unto my foe;
Nor to my departure owe
What my presence could not win.   60

"Absence is too much alone;
Better 'tis to go in peace,
Than my losses to increase
By a late fruitìon.

"Why should I enrich my fate?   65
'Tis a vanity to wear,
For my executioner,
Jewels of so high a rate.

"Rather I away will pine
In a manly stubbornness,   70
Than be fatted up express
For the cannibal to dine.

"Whilst this grief does thee disarm,
All th' enjoyment of our love
But the ravishment would prove   75
Of a body dead while warm.

"And I parting should appear
Like the gourmand Hebrew,° dead
While with° quails and manna fed,
He° does through the desert err;   80

"Or the witch that midnight wakes
For the fern, whose magic weed

---

78 gourmand Hebrew Numbers xi.33, where Jehovah having pro-
vided quails and manna strikes the Israelites "with a very great
plague"—presumably for eating greedily.   **79 with** Cooke; *he* in
1681.   **80 He** Cooke; *And* in *1681*.

In one minute casts the seed,°
And invisible him makes.

85   "Gentler times for love are meant;
      Who for parting pleasures strain
      Gather roses in the rain,
      Wet themselves and spoil their scent.

      "Farewell therefore all the fruit
90   Which I could from love receive:
      Joy will not with sorrow weave,
      Nor will I this grief pollute.

      "Fate, I come, as dark, as sad,
      As thy malice could desire;
95   Yet bring with me all the fire
      That love in his torches had."

      At these words away he broke;
      As who long has praying ly'n,
      To his headsman makes the sign,
100   And receives the parting stroke.

      But hence virgins all beware:
      Last night he with Phlogis slept;
      This night for Dorinda kept;
      And but rid to take the air.

105   Yet he does himself excuse,
      Nor indeed without a cause:
      For, according to the laws,
      Why did Chloë once refuse?

83 **seed** ferns having no seed; it was thought that they had, but
that the seed was invisible and could confer invisibility on anyone
who contrived to get hold of it. ("We have the receipt of fernseed,
we walk invisible," *1 Henry IV*, II.i.96.)

—

THE DEFINITION OF LOVE°

My Love is of a birth as rare
As 'tis for object strange and high:
It was begotten by Despair
Upon Impossibility.

Magnanimous Despair alone   5
Could show me so divine a thing,
Where feeble Hope could ne'er have flown,
But vainly flapped its tinsel wing.

And yet I quickly might arrive
Where my extended soul° is fixed,   10
But Fate does iron wedges drive,
And always crowds itself betwixt.

For Fate with jealous eye does see
Two perfect loves; nor lets them close:
Their union would her ruin be,   15
And her tyrannic power depose.

And therefore her decrees of steel
Us as the distant poles have placed
(Though Love's whole world on us doth wheel),
Not by themselves to be embraced: 20

Unless the giddy heaven fall,
And earth some new convulsion tear;

---

0 **The Definition of Love** This poem is discussed in the Introduction.   10 **extended soul** His soul resides in his mistress, not in him.

And, us to join, the world should all
Be cramped into a planisphere.°

25   As lines so loves oblique may well
Themselves in every angle greet:
But ours so truly parallel,
Though infinite can never meet.

Therefore the Love which us doth bind,
30   But Fate so enviously debars,
Is the conjunction of the mind,
And opposition° of the stars.

24 **planisphere** astrolabe, in which the poles are "clapt flat to-
gether" (the example of 1594 in *O.E.D.*). There is a possibility
(D. M. Schmitter, "The Cartography of 'The Definition of Love,'"
R.E.S. xii [1961], 49–51, and P. Legouis' partly dissenting com-
ment, 51–54) that the figure is terrestrial rather than celestial. Thus
the poles would be terrestrial, the planisphere a crushed globe,
with the lines of latitude parallel and those of longitude meeting at
the poles. Ann E. Berthoff (*R.E.S.* xvii [1966] 21–25 argues strongly
for the celestial interpretation.   31–32 **conjunction . . . opposition**
astrological terms, the first borrowed for the spiritual union of the
lovers, the second used also at a remove (the opposition is not
between the stars themselves but between the stars and the lovers).

THE PICTURE OF LITTLE T. C. IN A
PROSPECT OF FLOWERS°

See with what simplicity
This nymph begins her golden days!
In the green grass she loves to lie,
And there with her fair aspect tames
The wilder flowers, and gives them names:°   5
But only with the roses plays;
   And them does tell
What color best becomes them, and what smell.

Who can foretell for what high cause
This darling of the gods° was born!   10
Yet this is she whose chaster laws
The wanton Love shall one day fear,
And, under her command severe,
See his bow broke and ensigns torn.

0 **The Picture . . . Flowers** For an elaborate study of this poem, see Joseph H. Summers, "Marvell's 'Nature,'" *E.L.H.* xx (1953),121–35. Margoliouth suggested that T.C. was Theophila Cornewall, born 1644. A year earlier, the same parents had a child also christened Theophila who died at two days old. If, as Maren-Sofie Røstvig suggests (*Huntington Library Quarterly* xviii [1954–55] 13ff.), Marvell borrows from Benlowes' *Theophila*, and if E. E. Duncan-Jones is right in her subsequent conjecture (*H.L.Q.* xx [1956–57], 183–84) that in this title he takes over the literal sense of Benlowes (see note on l. 10), the poem is presumably later than 1652, the date of publication of Benlowes' book. Leishman, at considerable length, (pp. 165–89) traces the tradition of sub-amorous addresses to the pre-pubescent from the Greek Anthology through Horace to the poetry of Marvell's century and to Prior and Philips. Cf. *Young Love.* 5 **gives them names** a task traditionally attributed to Eve in Eden. 10 **darling of the gods** Theophila means "dear to the gods."

15   Happy, who can
Appease this virtuous enemy of man!

    O then let me in time compound,
    And parley with those conquering eyes;
    Ere they have tried their force to wound,
20   Ere, with their glancing wheels, they drive
    In triumph over hearts that strive,
    And them that yield but° more despise.
          Let me be laid,
Where I may see thy glories from some shade.

25   Meantime, whilst every verdant thing
    Itself does at thy beauty charm,
    Reform the errors of the spring;
    Make that the tulips may have share
    Of sweetness, seeing they are fair;
30   And roses of their thorns disarm:
          But most procure
That violets may a longer age endure.

    But O young beauty of the woods,
    Whom Nature courts with fruits and flowers,
35   Gather the flowers, but spare the buds;
    Lest Flora, angry at thy crime,
    To kill her infants in their prime,
    Do quickly make th' example yours;
          And, ere we see,
40   Nip in the blossom all our hopes and thee.

22 **but** only.

THE MATCH

Nature had long a treasure made
   Of all her choicest store;
Fearing, when she should be decayed,
   To beg in vain for more.

Her orientest colors there,   *5*
   And essences most pure,
With sweetest perfumes hoarded were,
   All, as she thought, secure.

She seldom them unlocked, or used,
   But with the nicest care;   *10*
For, with one grain of them diffused,
   She could the world repair.

But likeness soon together drew
   What she did separate lay;
Of which one perfect beauty grew,   *15*
   And that was Celia.

Love wisely had of long foreseen
   That he must once grow old;
And therefore stored a magazine,
   To save him from the cold.   *20*

He kept the several cells replete
   With niter thrice refined;
The naphtha's and the sulphur's heat,
   And all that burns the mind.

25   He fortified the double gate,
     And rarely thither came;
For, with one spark of these, he straight
     All Nature could inflame.

Till, by vicinity so long,
30   A nearer way they sought;
And, grown magnetically strong,
     Into each other wrought.

Thus, all his fuel did unite
     To make one fire high:
35   None ever burned so hot, so bright;
     And, Celia, that am I.

So we alone the happy rest,
     Whilst all the world is poor,
And have within ourselves possessed
40   All Love's and Nature's store.

THE MOWER AGAINST GARDENS°

Luxurious° man, to bring his vice in use,°
  Did after him the world seduce;
And from the fields the flowers and plants allure,
  Where Nature was most plain and pure.
He first enclosed within the garden's square   *5*
  A dead and standing pool of air:°
And a more luscious earth for them did knead,
  Which stupefied them while it fed.
The pink grew then as double as his mind;
  The nutriment did change the kind.   *10*
With strange perfumes he did the roses taint:
  And flowers themselves were taught to paint.
The tulip, white, did for complexion seek,
  And learned to interline its cheek;
Its onion root they then so high did hold,°   *15*
  That one was for a meadow sold.°

0 The Mower against Gardens This poem is more fully discussed
in the Introduction.   1 **Luxurious** sinful, lecherous.   1 **bring . . . use**
to reap interest on his vice.   6 **standing . . . air** Sir Henry Wotton's
Elements of Architecture (1624, reprinted 1651) says that one's
house ought to be "not unexercised, for want of wind: which were
to live, as it were, in a . . . standing pool of air" (Marcia E. Allen-
tuck, "Marvell's Pool of Air," *M.L.N.* lxxiv [1959]).   15 **hold** value.
16 **one . . . sold** Tulip bulbs were sold by weight in Holland during
the 1630s; one cost 5,500 florins or as much as 550 sheep (Mar-
goliouth). See Wilfrid Blunt, *Tulipomania* (1950).

Another world was searched, through oceans new,
　　To find the *Marvel of Peru.*°
And yet these rarities might be allowed
20　　To man, that sovereign thing and proud,
Had he not dealt between° the bark and tree,
　　Forbidden mixtures° there to see.
No plant now knew the stock from which it came;
　　He grafts upon the wild the tame,
25　That the uncertain and adult'rate fruit°
　　Might put the palate in dispute.
His green seraglio has its eunuchs too,
　　Lest any tyrant him outdo;
And in the cherry he does Nature vex,
30　　To procreate without a sex.°
'Tis all enforced; the fountain and the grot,
　　While the sweet fields do lie forgot:
Where willing Nature does to all dispense
　　A wild and fragrant innocence;
35　And fauns and fairies do the meadows till,
　　More by their presence than their skill.
Their statues, polished by some ancient hand,
　　May to adorn the gardens stand:
But howsoe'er the figures do excel,
40　　The gods themselves with us do dwell.

18 Marvel of Peru *Mirabilis Jalapa,* called by the botanist Parkinson (1629) *mirabilis peruviana,* "the Mervaile of Peru."　**21 dealt between** pandered for.　**22 forbidden mixtures** "Thou shalt not sow thy vineyard with divers seeds: lest the fruit of thy seed, which thou hast sown, and the fruit of thy vineyard, be defiled" (Deuteronomy, xxii, 91).　**25 uncertain . . . fruit** *pirus invito stipite mala tulit* ("the pear bore apples from its unwilling stock") Propertius, *Elegies,* IV, 2, 18.　**30 To . . . sex** explained by Hugh Macdonald as referring merely to propagation by grafting; but the proposal of M. C. Bradbrook and M. G. Lloyd Thomas, *Andrew Marvell* (1940), p. 40 n. 1—that the reference is to stoneless cherries —remains preferable; see Introduction.

DAMON THE MOWER

Hark how the Mower Damon sung,
With love of Juliana stung!
While everything did seem to paint
The scene more fit for his complaint:
Like her fair eyes the day was fair;   *5*
But scorching like his am'rous care:
Sharp like his scythe his sorrow was,
And withered like his hopes the grass.

"Oh what unusual heats are here,
Which thus our sunburned meadows sear!   *10*
The grasshopper its pipe gives o'er;
And hamstringed° frogs can dance no more:
But in the brook the green frog wades,
And grasshoppers seek out the shades.
Only the snake, that kept within,   *15*
Now glitters in its second skin.

"This heat the sun could never raise,
Nor Dog Star so inflames the days.
It from an higher beauty grow'th,
Which burns the fields and mower both: *20*
Which made the Dog,° and makes the sun
Hotter than his own Phaëton.°
Not July causeth these extremes,
But Juliana's scorching beams.

12 **hamstringed** lamed (by the heat).   21 **made the Dog** The annotated Oxford copy has *mads the Dog,* which may be right.
22 **Phaëton** the charioteer of the sun, who was unable to control it.

99

25   "Tell me where I may pass the fires
     Of the hot day, or hot desires.
     To what cool cave shall I descend,
     Or to what gelid fountain bend?
     Alas! I look for ease in vain,
30   When remedies themselves complain;
     No moisture but my tears do rest,
     Nor cold but in her icy breast.

     "How long wilt thou, fair Shepherdess,
     Esteem me, and my presents less?
35   To thee the harmless snake I bring,
     Disarmèd of its teeth and sting;
     To thee chameleons changing hue,
     And oak leaves tipped with honey dew.
     Yet thou, ungrateful, hast not sought
40   Nor what they are, nor who them brought.°

     "I am the Mower Damon, known
     Through all the meadows I have mown.
     On me the morn her dew distills
     Before her darling daffodils:
45   And, if at noon my toil me heat,
     The sun himself licks off my sweat;
     While, going home, the evening sweet
     In cowslip-water° bathes my feet.

35–40 **To thee . . . brought** The pastoral tradition of such gifts **as**
inducements to love begins, as Leishman points out, with those of
Polyphemus to Galatea in *Idyll* xi of Theocritus, elaborated by
Ovid in his Polyphemus-Galatea passage, *Metamorphoses* xiii,
798ff, and best known in Marlowe's *Passionate Shepherd to his
Love* (Leishman, 137). The closest parallel to Marlowe is probably
that in the famous Renaissance Latin poet Pontanus, *Lyra* xiii
(Polyphemus wooing). There is a particularly charming gift-
catalogue in Richard Barnefield's *Second Dayes Lamentation of
the Affectionate Shepheard* (1594) (*Poems*, ed. Grosart, 1876).
48 **cowslip-water** used by ladies to cleanse the skin.

"What though the piping shepherd stock
The plains with an unnumbered flock,   50
This scythe of mine discovers wide
More ground than all his sheep do hide.
With this the golden fleece I shear
Of all these closes° every year.
And though in wool more poor than they,   55
Yet am I richer far in hay.°

"Nor am I so deformed to sight,°
If in my scythe I lookèd right;
In which I see my picture done,
As in a crescent moon the sun.   60
The deathless fairies take me oft
To lead them in their dances soft;
And, when I tune myself to sing,
About me they contract their ring.°

"How happy might I still have mowed,   65
Had not Love here his thistles sowed!
But now I all the day complain,
Joining my labor to my pain;
And with my scythe cut down the grass,
Yet still my grief is where it was;   70
But, when the iron blunter grows,
Sighing I whet my scythe and woes."

While thus he threw his elbow round,
Depopulating all the ground,
And, with his whistling scythe, does cut   75
Each stroke between the earth and root,

49–56 **What . . . hay** The Mower is something of a novelty in
pastoral, but rivalry between rustics of different professions is not.
54 **closes** enclosed fields.   57 **Nor . . . sight** almost literally trans-
lated from Virgil *Eclogue* ii, 25: *nec sum adeo informis*. Leishman
rightly remarks that what is so characteristic of Marvell is to
transform this by having the speaker look not into a calm sea (as
Virgil's Corydon does) but into the curved and polished blade of
his scythe (p. 141).   64 **ring** the "fairy ring" which is actually
caused by the mycelium of certain fungi.

The edgèd steel by careless chance
Did into his own ankle glance;
And there among the grass fell down,
80 By his own scythe, the mower mown.

"Alas!" said he, "these hurts are slight
To those that die by Love's despite.
With shepherd's-purse,° and clown's-all-heal,°
The blood I staunch, and wound I seal.
85 Only for him no cure is found,
Whom Juliana's eyes do wound.
'Tis death alone that this must do:
For Death, thou art a Mower too."

---

83 **shepherd's purse** *capsella bursa-pastoris*, a weed supposed to check bleeding.   83 **clown's-all-heal** *stachys palustris*, said to heal wounds.

THE MOWER TO THE GLOWWORMS

Ye living lamps,° by whose dear light
The nightingale does sit so late,
And studying all the summer-night,
Her matchless songs does meditate;

Ye country comets, that portend   5
No war, nor prince's funeral,
Shining unto no higher end
Than to presage the grass's fall;°

Ye glowworms, whose officious° flame
To wand'ring mowers shows the way,   10
That in the night have lost their aim,
And after foolish fires° do stray;

Your courteous lights in vain you waste,
Since Juliana here is come,
For she my mind hath so displaced   15
That I shall never find my home.

---

1 **lamps** "You will make me believe that glow-worms are lanterns"—
this proverb (Tilley G 134) is cited by Kitty Scoular, *Natural Magic*,
1965, p. 103. 7–8 **Shining . . . fall** "glowbands never appear be-
fore hay is ripe, upon the ground, nor yet after it is cut down"
(Pliny, *Natural History* XI, xxviii, translated by Philemon Holland;
quoted by Leishman, p. 152). Kitty Scoular (p. 107) points to an
exact parallel in Remy Belleau, for whom the insect is also the
countryman's prophet:

> Qui au laboureur prophétise
> Qu'il faut pour faucher agnise
> Sa faulx, et face les moissons.

9 **officious** attentive   12 **foolish fires** *ignis fatuus*, will-o'-the-wisp;
marsh-gas (methane) spontaneously ignited.

THE MOWER'S SONG

My mind was once the true survey°
Of all these meadows fresh and gay;
And in the greenness of the grass
Did see its hopes as in a glass;°
5   When Juliana came, and she
What I do to the grass, does to my thoughts and me.

But these, while I with sorrow pine,
Grew more luxuriant still and fine;
That not one blade of grass you spied,
10   But had a flower on either side;
When Juliana came, and she
What I do to the grass, does to my thoughts and me.

Unthankful meadows, could you so
A fellowship so true forgo,
15   And in your gaudy May-games meet,
While I lay trodden under feet?
When Juliana came, and she
What I do to the grass, does to my thoughts and me.

But what you in compassion ought,
20   Shall now by my revenge be wrought;
And flowers, and grass, and I and all,
Will in one common ruin fall.
For Juliana comes, and she
What I do to the grass, does to my thoughts and me.

25   And thus, ye meadows, which have been
Companions of my thoughts more green,
Shall now the heraldry become
With which I shall adorn my tomb;
For Juliana comes, and she
30   What I do to the grass, does to my thoughts and me.

---

1 **survey** account, as might be given by a surveyor. 3–4 **in … glass.**
Green was traditionally the color of hope.

AMETAS AND THESTYLIS MAKING HAY-ROPES

Ametas.   Think'st thou that this love can stand,
             Whilst thou still dost say me nay?
             Love unpaid does soon disband;
             Love binds love as hay binds hay.

Thestylis. Think'st thou that this rope would twine   5
             If we both should turn one way?
             Where both parties so combine,
             Neither love will twist nor hay.

Ametas.   Thus you vain excuses find,
             Which yourself and us delay;   10
             And love ties a woman's mind
             Looser than with ropes of hay.

Thestylis. What you cannot constant hope
             Must be taken as you may.

Ametas.   Then let's both lay by our rope,   15
             And go kiss within the hay.

MUSIC'S EMPIRE°

First was the world as one great cymbal made,
Where jarrring winds to infant Nature played.
All music was a solitary sound,
To hollow rocks and murm'ring fountains bound.

5 Jubal° first made the wilder notes agree;
And Jubal tunèd music's Jubilee;°
He called the echoes from their sullen° cell,
And built the organ's city where they dwell.

Each sought a consort in that lovely place,
10 And virgin trebles wed the manly bass.
From whence the progeny of numbers new
Into harmonious colonies withdrew.

Some to the lute, some to the viol went,
And others chose the cornet eloquent.
15 These practicing the wind, and those the wire,
To sing men's triumphs, or in Heaven's choir.

Then music, the mosaic° of the air,
Did of all these a solemn noise prepare;
With which she gained the empire of the ear,
20 Including all between the earth and sphere.

Victorious sounds! yet here your homage do
Unto a gentler conqueror° than you;
Who though he flies the music of his praise,
Would with you Heaven's Hallelujahs raise.

0 **Music's Empire** This poem is a variant of the traditional *laus musi-
cae*, for which see James Hutton, "Some English Poems in Praise
of Music," *English Miscellany* (Rome) II (1951), 1–63. For an
elaborate study of its deviations from this norm, and its relation to
musica speculativa and *musica instrumentalis*, see John Hollander,
The Untuning of the Sky (1961) pp. 309–315. 5 **Jubal** "the father
of all such as handle the harp and organ" (Gen. iv. 21). He was
the Christian equivalent of the pagan originators of music, Orpheus
and Amphion. 6 **Jubilee** time of rejoicing; but Marvell may have
been thinking of the ram's horn which signaled the Hebrew jubilee.
7 **sullen** solitary, lonely. 17 **mosaic** presenting a unity made up of
diverse sound. 22 **conqueror** Margoliouth suggests Fairfax, com-
paring the following line with *Upon the Hill and Grove at Bilbrough,*
lines 75–6: Hollander (314) argues for Cromwell.

THE GARDEN°

How vainly men themselves amaze
To win the palm, the oak, or bays;°
And their uncessant labors see
Crowned from some single herb or tree:
Whose short and narrow vergèd shade   5
Does prudently their toils upbraid;
While all flowers and all° trees do close
To weave the garlands of repose.

Fair Quiet, have I found thee here,
And Innocence, thy sister dear!   10
Mistaken long, I sought you then
In busy companies of men.
Your sacred plants, if here below,
Only among the plants° will grow.
Society is all but rude,   15
To this delicious solitude.°

No white nor red° was ever seen
So am'rous as this lovely green.°

0 **The Garden** This poem is discussed in the Introduction. The Latin
version *Hortus*, which also appears in *1681*, is not throughout a
translation, nor yet an original, but partly an exercise in a related
mode (see G. Williamson, "Marvell's 'Hortus' and 'Garden,'" in
Milton and Others, 1965).   2 **the palm . . . bays** rewards for achieve
ment in war, statesmanship, poetry.   7 **all . . . all** as opposed to the
"single" of line 4; retirement offers greater rewards.   14 **plants** i.e.,
the plants symbolizing them, as palm, oak and bays, symbolize the
various activities of line 2.   15–16 **Society . . . solitude**. a paradox:
ordinarily it is society that is thought of as "polished."   17 **white
. . . red** emblematic of female beauty.   18 **green** by association,
emblematic of rural and solitary retirement.

Fond lovers, cruel as their flame,
20 Cut in these trees their mistress' name.
Little, alas, they know, or heed,
How far these beauties hers exceed!
Fair Trees! wheres'e'er your barks I wound,
No names shall but your own° be found.

25 When we have run our passion's heat,°
Love hither makes his best retreat.°
The gods, that mortal beauty chase,
Still° in a tree did end their race:
Apollo hunted Daphne so,
30 Only that she might laurel grow;
And Pan did after Syrinx speed,
Not as a nymph, but for a reed.°

What wond'rous life is° this I lead!
Ripe apples drop about my head;
35 The luscious clusters of the vine
Upon my mouth do crush their wine;
The nectarine, and curious peach,
Into my hands themselves do reach;
Stumbling on melons, as I pass,
40 Ensnared with flowers, I fall on grass.°

24 **No . . . own** If lovers behave thus to celebrate women's beauty, it is logical—since the trees are more beautiful than the women—to carve only the tree's name on the tree.   25 **heat** (1) ardor (2) race. 26 **retreat** (1) a military and (2) a religious figure.   28 **Still** always. 29–32 **Apollo . . . reed** In the myth, Apollo is thwarted when Daphne turns into a laurel and Pan when Syrinx turns into a reed; Marvell inverts the myths to establish the "amorous" superiority of trees to women.   33 **is** in *1681*.   33–40 **What . . . grass** In this paradise, as in that of Adam, one is exposed to all sensual delight, but here one can be ensnared and fall without serious consequences. The catalogue of readily available fruit is a commonplace with a long history.

Meanwhile the mind, from pleasure less,°
Withdraws into its happiness:
The mind, that ocean° where each kind
Does straight its own resemblance find;
Yet it creates, transcending these,   45
Far other worlds, and other seas;°
Annihilating all that's made
To a green thought in a green shade.°

Here at the fountain's sliding foot,
Or at some fruit-tree's mossy root,   50
Casting the body's vest aside,
My soul into the boughs does glide:
There like a bird it sits, and sings,
Then whets,° and combs its silver wings;
And, till prepared for longer flight,°   55
Waves in its plumes the various light.°

Such was that happy Garden-state,
While man there walked without a mate:°
After a place so pure, and sweet,
What other help could yet be meet!°   60

41 from . . . less experiencing less pleasure in nature than the delighted senses do (and so turning upwards).   43 that ocean alluding to the belief that there is in the sea a parallel creation for everything on land. The implied theory of knowledge is that we can know the world because of the pre-existence of related forms in our minds.   45–46 Yet . . . seas But the mind does more than merely provide such correspondences; the fancy or imagination can create forms which have no equivalent in reality.   47–48 Annihilating . . . shade making the created world seem as nothing compared with what can be imagined by the retired contemplative.   54 whets preens.   55 Till . . . flight resting, as it were, between the created and the intelligible worlds in the process of its Platonic ascent; the same figure in the same context is used by Spenser, Hymn of Heavenly Beauty, lines 22–28.   56 various light The Neo-platonic image of the white light of eternity broken into color in the temporal world (familiar to all from Adonais) was common enough in the Renaissance: see, e.g., Chapman, Ovid's Banquet of Sense, st. 55.   57-58 Such . . . mate The Garden of Eden was like this before the introduction of Eve; a point earlier made by St. Ambrose (Epist. I, 49). 60 help . . . meet "And the Lord God said, It is not good that the man should be alone; I will make him an help meet for him" (Gen. 2, 18).

But 'twas beyond a mortal's share
To wander solitary there:
Two paradises 'twere in one
To live in paradise alone.

65   How well the skillful gard'ner drew
Of flowers and herbs this dial° new;
Where from above the milder sun
Does through a fragrant° zodiac run;
And, as it works, th' industrious bee
70   Computes its time° as well as we.
How could such sweet and wholesome hours
Be reckoned but with herbs and flowers!

66 **dial** sundial (here the garden itself).   67–68 **milder ... fragrant**
The sun is made milder because in this "floral zodiac" the sunlight is
filtered through trees, on to plants.   70 **time** a pun: the clock
enables us to tell the time and enables the bee to take nectar from
thyme. Marvel gets this point into his Latin version also.

A TRANSLATION OF THE SECOND CHORUS FROM SENECA'S *THYESTES*

Climb at Court for me that will,
Tott'ring favor's pinnacle;
All I seek is to lie still.
Settled in some secret nest
In calm leisure let me rest;   5
And far off the public stage
Pass away my silent age.
Thus when without noise, unknown,
I have lived out all my span,
I shall die, without a groan,   10
An old honest country man.
Who exposed to others' eyes,
Into his own heart ne'er pries,
Death to him's a strange surprise.

AN EPITAPH UPON ——

Enough: and leave the rest to Fame.
'Tis to commend her but to name.
Courtship, which living she declined,
When dead to offer were unkind.
5 Where never any could speak ill,
Who would officious praises spill?
Nor can the truest wit or friend,
Without detracting, her commend.
To say she lived a virgin chaste,
10 In this age loose and all unlaced;
Nor was, when vice is so allowed,
Of virtue or ashamed, or proud;
That her soul was on Heav'n so bent
No minute but it came and went;°
15 That ready her last debt to pay
She summed her life up every day;
Modest as morn; as mid-day bright;
Gentle as ev'ning; cool as night;
'Tis true: but all so weakly said;
20 'Twere more significant: "she's dead."

14 **came and went** i.e., in prayer.

UPON THE HILL AND GROVE AT BILBROUGH°

TO THE LORD FAIRFAX

See how the archèd earth does here
Rise in a perfect hemisphere!
The stiffest compass could not strike
A line more circular and like,
Nor softest pencil draw a brow   5
So equal as this hill does bow.
It seems as for a model° laid,
And that the world by it was made.

Here learn, ye mountains more unjust,
Which to abrupter greatness thrust,   10
That do with your hook-shouldered height
The earth deform and heaven fright,
For° whose excrescence ill-designed,
Nature must a new center° find,

---

0 **Upon . . . Bilbrough** For similar poems on mountains, see Kitty
Scoular, *Natural Magic*, 154ff. In part an exercise in a manner
much more fully developed in *Upon Appleton House*. Bilbrough
was a house of Fairfax's near Nun Appleton. Thomas Fairfax (1612–
1671), the third baron, had been commander-in-chief of the Par-
liamentary Army. He refused to condone the execution of the
King and resigned in June 1650 because he disapproved of the
proposed campaign against the Scots, which Cromwell undertook.
Fairfax then retired to his Yorkshire properties, where he led the
life of the great landowner who was also a scholar and a poet. He
had married Ann Vere, who came from a distinguished military
family, in 1637; she appears to have been an imposing woman of
strong Presbyterian faith. In 1651, they appointed Marvell tutor
to their daughter Mary, and he appears to have remained with
them at Nun Appleton and Bilbrough for two years. Related to
this poem is the Latin *Epigramma in duos montes* printed before
it in *1681*. 7 **model** i.e., in its perfect circularity. 13 **For** on
account of. 14 **new center** because the irregularity of the moun-
tains has made the earth imperfectly spherical.

15   Learn here those humble steps to tread,
      Which to securer glory lead.

      See what a soft access and wide
      Lies open to its grassy side;
      Nor with the rugged path deters
20   The feet of breathless travelers.
      See then how courteous it ascends,
      And all the way it rises bends;
      Nor for itself the height does gain,
      But only strives to raise the plain.

25   Yet thus it all the field commands,
      And in unenvied greatness stands,
      Discerning further than the cliff
      Of heaven-daring Teneriffe.°
      How glad the weary seamen° haste
30   When they salute it from the mast!
      By night the northern star their way
      Directs, and this no less by day.

      Upon its crest this mountain grave
      A plump° of agèd trees does wave.
35   No hostile hand durst ere invade
      With impious steel the sacred° shade,
      For something always did appear
      Of the great master's terror° there;
      And men could hear his armor still
40   Rattling through all the grove and hill.

      Fear of the master, and respect
      Of the great nymph did it protect;
      Vera° the nymph that him inspired,
      To whom he often here retired,
45   And on these oaks engraved her name;
      Such wounds alone these woods became;

---

28 Teneriffe volcanic peak in Canary Islands (12,192 ft). Bilbrough
Hill is 145 feet.   **29 seamen** They used the hill as a landmark for
entering the Humber.   **34 plump** clump.   **36 sacred** Clumps of
trees so placed were often thought of as sacred groves.   **38 great
. . . terror** the authority of Fairfax.   **43 Vera** Ann Vere, Lady
Fairfax.

But ere he well the barks could part
'Twas writ already in their heart.

For they ('tis credible) have sense,
As we, of love and reverence,   *50*
And underneath the coarser rind
The genius of the house do bind.
Hence they successes seem to know,
And in their Lord's advancement grow;
But in no memory were seen   *55*
As under this° so straight and green.

Yet now no further strive to shoot,
Contented if they fix their root;
Nor to the wind's uncertain gust,
Their prudent heads too far intrust.   *60*
Only sometimes a flutt'ring breeze
Discourses with the breathing trees;
Which in their modest whispers name
Those acts that swelled the cheek of Fame.

"Much other groves," say they, "than these,   *65*
And other hills him once did please.
Through groves of pikes he thundered then,
And mountains raised of dying men.
For all the civic garlands due
To him our branches are but few.   *70*
Nor are our trunks enough to bear
The trophies of one fertile year."

'Tis true, ye trees, nor ever spoke
More certain oracles in oak.°
But peace (if you his favor prize),   *75*
That courage its own praises flies.
Therefore to your obscurer seats
From his own brightness he retreats:
Nor he the hills without the groves,
Nor height but with retirement loves.   *80*

---

56 **this** i.e., this lord.   74 **oak** referring to the sacred oak at Dodona, from the rustling of whose leaves the will of Zeus could be discovered.

UPON APPLETON HOUSE°

TO MY LORD FAIRFAX

Within this sober frame expect
Work of no foreign architect,
That unto caves the quarries drew,
And forests did to pastures hew;
Who of his great design in pain
Did for a model vault his brain,°
Whose columns should so high be raised
To arch the brows that on them gazed.°

0 **Upon Appleton House** This poem is discussed in the Introduction, but some aspects are more conveniently dealt with here. For Fairfax and his wife, see note to previous poem. Appleton House was a brick mansion with a center block and two wings at right-angles, forming three sides of a square. "The great hall or gallery occupied the centre between the two wings. It was fifty yards long . . . the central part of the house was surrounded by a cupola . . . A noble park with splendid oak-trees, and containing 300 head of deer, stretched away to the north, while on the south side were the ruins of the old Nunnery, the flower-garden, and the low meadows called *ings* extending to the banks of the Wharfe. . . . The flowers were planted in masses, tulips, pinks and roses, each in separate beds, which were cut into the shape of forts with five bastions" (C. R. Markham, *Life of the Great Lord Fairfax*, 1870, p. 365). How much this account owes to the poem is not known. The first Nun Appleton House belonged to a Cistercian Priory, and was acquired by the Fairfaxes at the dissolution in 1542. The house in which Marvell lived was built between 1637 and 1650. The wings have gone, and the rest is much altered; some nunnery ruins remain. Marvell's poem is a somewhat anomalous member of a considerable class of poems about country houses and their lords; see Introduction. 1–8 **Within . . . gazed** This somewhat chauvinistic praise for the modesty of Nun Appleton is probably intended to be a criticism of poems praising the architectural grandeur of a patron's house; specifically, perhaps, of Saint Amant's praise of the Duc de Retz's hunting lodge in his *Palais de la Volupté:* "L'invention en est nouvelle, / Et ne vient que d'une cervelle / Qui fait tout avec tant de poids, / Et prend de tout si bien le chois / Qu'elle met en claire evidence / Que sa grandeur et sa prudence / Sont aussi dignes, sans mentir, / De regner comme de bastir." 5–6 **Who . . . brain** who, in agony to realize his great design, employed his skull as a model for the vault.

Why should of all things man unruled
Such unproportioned dwellings build?   10
The beasts are by their dens expressed,
And birds contrive an equal° nest;
The low-roofed tortoises do dwell
In cases fit of tortoise-shell.
No creature loves an empty space;   15
Their bodies measure out their place.

But he, superfluously spread,
Demands more room alive than dead;
And in his hollow palace goes
Where winds as he themselves may lose.   20
What need of all this marble crust
T' impark the wanton mote of dust,
That thinks by breadth the world t' unite
Though the first builders° failed in height?

But all things are composèd here   25
Like Nature, orderly and near:
In which we the dimensions find
Of that more sober age and mind,
When larger sizèd men did stoop
To enter at a narrow loop;   30
As practicing, in doors so strait,
To strain themselves through Heaven's gate.

And surely when the after age
Shall hither come in pilgrimage,
These sacred places to adore,   35
By Vere° and Fairfax trod before,
Men will dispute how their extent
Within such dwarfish confines went;
And some will smile at this as well
As Romulus his bee-like cell.°   40

12 **equal** appropriate (to their size).   24 **the first builders** the build-
ers of the tower of Babel, Gen. xi.   36 **Vere** Ann Vere, Fairfax's
wife.   40 **Romulus . . . cell** the thatched hut, in which Romulus,
founder of Rome, had lived, was compared to a beehive.

Humility alone designs
Those short but admirable lines,
By which, ungirt and unconstrained,
Things greater are in less contained.
45   Let other vainly strive t' immure
The circle in the quadrature!°
These holy mathematics can
In every figure equal man.

Yet thus the laden house does sweat,
50   And scarce endures the master great:
But where he comes the swelling hall
Stirs, and the square grows spherical;°
More by his magnitude distressed,
Than he is by its straitness pressed;
55   And too officiously it slights
That° in itself which him delights.

So honor better lowness bears,
Than that unwonted greatness wears;
Height with a certain grace does bend,
60   But low things clownishly ascend.
And yet what needs there here excuse,
Where every thing does answer use?
Where neatness nothing can condemn,
Nor pride invent° what to contemn?

65   A stately frontispiece of poor°
Adorns without the open door;
Nor less the rooms within commends
Daily new furniture of friends.

---

46 **The circle . . . quadrature** a reference to the old problem of
squaring the circle; for an interesting account, see R. I. Colie, "Some
Paradoxes in the Language of Things," in *Reason and the Imagina-
tion,* ed. J. A. Mazzeo, New York, 1962, pp. 121–23. The problem
"became the standard trope for time-wasting intellectual activity."
But to live by the square of human constancy, and respect the circle
of heaven (the circle a symbol for God) is "holy mathematics."
52 **spherical** a reference to the cupola.   56 **That** its humility.
64 **invent** find out.   65 **frontispiece of poor** The door is conceived
as the frontispiece of a book and the poor, confidently expecting
the alms of Fairfax, are its decoration.

The house was built upon the place
Only as for a mark of grace;   *70*
And for an inn° to entertain
Its Lord awhile, but not remain.

Him Bishops-Hill,° or Denton° may,
Or Bilbrough, better hold than they;
But Nature here hath been so free   *75*
As if she said, "Leave this to me."
Art would more neatly have defaced
What she had laid so sweetly waste;
In fragrant gardens, shady woods,
Deep meadows, and transparent floods.   *80*

While with slow eyes we these survey,
And on each pleasant footstep stay,
We opportunely may relate
The progress of this house's fate.
A nunnery first gave it birth   *85*
(For virgin buildings oft brought forth);
And all that neighbor-ruin shows
The quarries whence this dwelling rose.

Near to this gloomy cloister's gates
There dwelt the blooming virgin Thwaites;°   *90*
Fair beyond measure, and an heir
Which might deformity make fair.
And oft she spent the summer suns
Discoursing with the subtle nuns;
Whence in these words one to her weaved   *95*
(As 'twere by chance) thoughts long conceived.

---

71 **inn** a reference to some lines of Fairfax, preserved in the
Bodleian, called *Upon the New-built House at Appleton:* "Think
not, O man, / that dwells herein / This house a stay but as an
inn / Which for convenience fitly stands / In way to one not
made with hands." 73 **Bishops-Hill** Fairfax's house in York.
73 **Denton** another Fairfax estate thirty miles from Nun Appleton.
90 **Thwaites** Isabella Thwaites married an ancestor of Fairfax. She
had been left in the charge of the Prioress of Nun Appleton, who
tried, by shutting her up, to prevent her marriage to Sir William
Fairfax; but her authority was overridden, and the marriage took
place in 1518.

"Within this holy leisure we
Live innocently as you see.
These walls restrain the world without,
100   But hedge our liberty about:
These bars inclose that wider den
Of those wild ceatures, callèd men;
The cloister outward shuts its gates,
And, from us, locks on them the grates.

105   "Here we, in shining armor white,°
Like virgin Amazons do fight:
And our chaste lamps we hourly trim,
Lest the great Bridegroom find them dim.°
Our orient breaths perfumèd are
110   With incense of incessant prayer:
And holy-water of our tears
Most strangely our complexion clears:

"Not tears of grief; but such as those
With which calm pleasure overflows;
115   Or pity, when we look on you
That live without this happy vow.
How should we grieve that must be seen
Each one a Spouse, and each a Queen;
And can in Heaven hence behold
120   Our brighter robes and crowns of gold?

"When we have prayèd all our beads,
Someone the holy legend reads;
While all the rest with needles paint
The face and graces of the saint.
125   But what the linen can't receive
They in their lives do interweave;
This work the saints best represents;
That serves for altar's ornaments.

"But much it to our work would add
130   If here your hand, your face we had.
By it we would Our Lady touch;

105 **white** the color of the Cistercian habit.   107-08 **our . . . dim**
referring to the parable of the wise and foolish virgins, Matt. xxv.

Yet thus She you resembles much.
Some of your features, as we sewed,
Through every shrine should be bestowed:
And in one beauty we would take   *135*
Enough a thousand saints to make.

"And (for I dare not quench the fire
That me does for your good inspire)
'Twere sacrilege a man t' admit
To holy things, for Heaven fit.   *140*
I see the angels in a crown°
On you the lilies show'ring down;
And round about you glory breaks,
That something more than human speaks.

"All beauty, when at such a height,   *145*
Is so already consecrate.
Fairfax I know; and long ere this
Have marked the youth, and what he is.
But can he such a rival seem
For whom you Heav'n should disesteem?   *150*
Ah, no! and 'twould more honor prove
He your *devoto*° were, than love.

"Here live belovèd, and obeyed,
Each one your sister, each your maid.
And, if our rule seem strictly penned,   *155*
The rule itself to you shall bend.
Our Abbess too, now far in age,
Doth your succession near presage.
How soft the yoke on us would lie,
Might such fair hands as yours it tie!   *160*

"Your voice, the sweetest of the choir,
Shall draw Heav'n nearer, raise us higher:
And your example, if our head,
Will soon us to perfection lead.
Those virtues to us all so dear,   *165*
Will straight grow sanctity when here:
And that, once sprung, increase so fast
Till miracles it work at last.

141 **crown** of lilies (next line).   152 **devoto** devotee.

    "Nor is our order yet so nice,
170 Delight to banish as a vice.
    Here pleasure piety doth meet,
    One perfecting the other sweet;
    So through the mortal fruit we boil
    The sugar's uncorrupting oil;
175 And that which perished while we pull,
    Is thus preservèd clear and full.

    "For such indeed are all our arts;
    Still handling Nature's finest parts.
    Flowers dress the altars; for the clothes,
180 The sea-born amber° we compose;
    Balms for the grieved° we draw; and pastes
    We mold, as baits for curious tastes.
    What need is here of man? unless
    These as sweet sins we should confess.

185 "Each night among us to your side
    Appoint a fresh and virgin bride,
    Whom if Our Lord at midnight find,
    Yet neither should be left behind;
    Where you may lie as chaste in bed,
190 As pearls together billeted;
    All night embracing arm in arm,
    Like crystal pure in cotton warm.

    "But what is this to all the store
    Of joys you see, and may make more!
195 Try but a while, if you be wise;
    The trial neither costs, nor ties."
    Now, Fairfax, seek her promised faith!
    Religion that dispensèd hath;
    Which she henceforward does begin:°
200 The nun's smooth tongue has sucked her in.

---

180 **sea-born amber** ambergris (see *Bermudas* l. 28) used to per-
fume linen in storage.   181 **grieved** hurt, wounded.   197–99 **Now
. . . begin** These obscure lines appear to mean: Fairfax, now is the
time to seek her pledge, since she has been released from her
religious obligations; but she nevertheless embarks upon the
religious life.

Oft, though he knew it was in vain,
Yet would he valiantly complain:
"Is this that sanctity so great,
An art by which you finelier cheat?
Hypocrite witches, hence *avant*,°   205
Who though in prison yet enchant!
Death only can such thieves make fast,
As rob though in the dungeon cast.

"Were there but, when this house was made,
One stone that a just hand had laid,   210
It must have fall'n upon her head
Who first thee from thy faith misled.
And yet, how well soever meant,
With them 'twould soon grow fraudulent:
For like themselves they alter all,   215
And vice infects the very wall.°

"But sure those buildings last not long,
Founded by folly, kept by wrong.
I know what fruit their gardens yield,
When they it think by night concealed.   220
Fly from their vices. 'Tis thy state,°
Not thee, that they would consecrate.
Fly from their ruin. How I fear
Though guiltless lest thou perish there!"

What should he do? He would respect   225
Religion, but not right neglect;
For first religion taught him right,
And dazzled not but cleared his sight.
Sometimes resolved his sword he draws,
But reverenceth then the laws: 230
For Justice still that Courage led;
First from a judge, then soldier° bred.

205 **avant** avaunt.   216 **vice . . . wall** So that the stone, even though
laid by a just hand, would not fall on the girl's seducer, simply
because it has been infected by the vice of the inmates of the
nunnery.   221 **state** estate, property.   232 **judge . . . soldier** Sir
William Fairfax's father was a judge, his mother the daughter of
Lord Roos, a distinguished soldier.

Small honor would be in the storm.°
The Court him grants the lawful form;
235 Which licensed either peace or force,
To hinder the unjust divorce.
Yet still the nuns his right debarred,
Standing upon their holy guard.
Ill-counseled women, do you know
240 Whom you resist, or what you do?

Is not this he whose offspring fierce
Shall fight through all the universe;
And with successive valor try
France, Poland, either Germany;°
245 Till one,° as long since prophesied,
His horse through conquered Britain ride?
Yet, against fate, his spouse they kept,
And the great race would intercept.°

Some to the breach against their foes
250 Their wooden saints in vain oppose.
Another bolder stands at push
With their old holy-water brush.
While the disjointed° Abbess threads
The jingling chain-shot of her beads.
255 But their loud'st cannon were their lungs;
And sharpest weapons were their tongues.

But, waving these aside like flies,
Young Fairfax through the wall does rise.
Then th' unfrequented vault appeared,
260 And superstitions vainly feared.
The relics false were set to view;
Only the jewels there were true—
But truly bright and holy Thwaites
That weeping at the altar waits.

233 **in the storm** in taking her from the nunnery by force.
241-44 **Is . . . Germany** Sir Thomas, son of this pair, fought in
Germany and his son in France; son of the next generation fought
in Germany and was Marvell's patron in France.   245 **one** some fu-
ture descendant. Nothing is known of the prophecy.   248 **would in-
tercept** wished to interrupt (the family succession).   253 **disjointed**
distracted.

But the glad youth away her bears   *265*
And to the nuns bequeaths her tears:
Who guiltily their prize bemoan,
Like gypsies that a child hath stol'n.
Thenceforth (as when th' enchantment ends
The castle vanishes or rends)   *270*
The wasting cloister with the rest
Was in one instant dispossessed.

At the demolishing, this seat
To Fairfax fell as by escheat.°
And what both nuns and founders willed   *275*
'Tis likely better thus fulfilled:
For if the virgin proved not theirs,
The cloister yet remainèd hers;
Though many'a nun there made her vow,
'Twas no *religious house* till now.   *280*

From that blest bed the hero° came,
Whom France and Poland yet does fame;
Who, when retirèd here to peace,
His warlike studies could not cease;
But laid these gardens out in sport   *285*
In the just figure of a fort;
And with five bastions it did fence,
As aiming one for every sense.°

When in the east the morning ray
Hangs out the colors of the day,   *290*
The bee through these known alleys hums,
Beating the *dian*° with its drums.
Then flowers their drowsy eyelids raise,
Their silken ensigns each displays,
And dries its pan° yet dank with dew,   *295*
And fills its flask° with odors new.

---

274 **escheat** a legal term: if the tenant died without an heir, the
estate reverted to the lord.   281–82 **hero** It is uncertain whether
he means Sir Thomas Fairfax, son of this marriage, or Lord
Fairfax, Marvell's employer.   288 **every sense** There were gardens
so laid out in sixteenth-century France.   292 **dian** reveille.   295 **pan**
the part of the musket lock holding the priming.   296 **flask** powder-
flask. (The flowers represented as infantrymen.)

These, as their governor goes by,
In fragrant volleys they let fly;
And to salute their governess
300 Again as great a charge they press:
None for the virgin nymph;° for she
Seems with the flowers a flower to be.
And think° so still! though not compare°
With breath so sweet, or cheek so fair.

305 Well shot ye firemen!° Oh how sweet,
And round your equal fires do meet;
Whose shrill report no ear can tell,
But echoes to the eye and smell.
See how the flowers, as at parade,
310 Under their colors stand displayed:
Each regiment in order grows,
That of the tulip, pink, and rose.

But when the vigilant patrol
Of stars walks round about the pole,
315 Their leaves, that to the stalks are curled
Seem to their staves the ensigns furled.
Then in some flower's belovèd hut
Each bee as sentinel is shut;
And sleeps so too: but, if once stirred,
320 She runs you through, nor° asks the word.

Oh thou, that dear and happy isle
The garden of the world° ere while,
Thou paradise of foùr° seas,
Which Heaven planted us to please,
325 But to exclude the world, did guard
With wat'ry if not flaming sword;

---

301 **virgin nymph** Mary Fairfax.   303 **think** imperative, addressed
to the flowers.   303 **not compare** do not invite comparison with.
305 **firemen** soldiers using firearms (as distinct, for example, from
bowmen).   320 **nor** Cooke; *or in 1681*. If the *1681* reading is right,
or must mean *"ere"*—"before asking the password."   322 **garden
of the world** For this familiar topic (England as garden of the
world) see J. W. Bennett, "Britain among the Fortunate Isles,"
S.P. liii (1956), pp. 114ff., and Leishman, pp. 283ff.   323 **foùr** (a
disyllable).

What luckless apple did we taste,
To make us mortal, and thee waste?

Unhappy! shall we never more
That sweet militia° restore,   *330*
When gardens only had their towers,
And all the garrisons were flowers;
When roses only arms might bear,
And men did rosy garlands wear?
Tulips, in several colors barred,   *335*
Were then the Switzers° of our Guard.

The gardener had the soldier's place,
And his more gentle forts did trace.
The nursery of all things green
Was then the only magazine.   *340*
The winter quarters were the stoves
Where he the tender plants removes.
But war all this doth overgrow;
We ordnance plant, and power sow.

And yet there walks one on the sod   *345*
Who, had it pleasèd him and God,
Might once have made our gardens spring
Fresh as his own and flourishing.
But he preferred to the *Cinque Ports*°
These five imaginary forts;   *350*
And, in those half-dry trenches, spanned°
Power which the ocean might command.

For he did, with his utmost skill,
Ambition weed, but Conscience till—
Conscience, that Heaven-nursèd plant,   *355*
Which most our earthly gardens want.°
A prickling leaf it bears, and such

---

330 **militia** (four syllables).   336 **Switzers** referring to the black, yellow and red stripes of the papal Swiss Guard.   349 **Cinque Ports** a group of ancient ports on the southeast coast of England. Their Wardenship was an important military appointment (later it became purely ceremonial, as when Sir Winston Churchill held it). Fairfax was Warden 1650–1651.   351 **spanned** confined.   356 **want** lack.

As that which shrinks° at every touch;
But flowers eternal, and divine,
360 That in the crowns of saints do shine.

The sight does from these bastions ply
Th' invisible artillery;
And at proud Cawood Castle° seems
To point the batt'ry of its beams,
365 As if it quarreled° in the seat
Th' ambition of its prelate great;
But o'er the meads below it plays,
Or innocently seems to gaze.

And now to the abyss I pass
370 Of that unfathomable grass,
Where men like grasshoppers appear,
But grasshoppers are giants° there:
They, in their squeaking laugh, contemn
Us as we walk more low than them;
375 And, from the precipices tall
Of the green spires, to us do call.

To see men through this meadow dive
We wonder how they rise alive;
As, under water, none does know
380 Whether he fall through it or go;
But as the mariners that sound
And show upon their lead the ground,°
They bring up flowers so to be seen,
And prove they've at the bottom been.

385 No scene that turns with engines strange°
Does oft'ner than these meadows change:

358 **shrinks** the sensitive plant.   363 **Cawood Castle** until 1642, a
seat of the Archbishop of York, about two miles from Nun
Appleton.   365 **quarreled** found fault with.   372 **giants** "And there
we saw the giants . . . and we were in our own sight as grasshoppers,
and so were we in their sight" (Numbers xiii, 33).   382 **the ground**
mud or sand from the seabed.   385 **scene . . . strange** referring to
the elaborate machinery of the Renaissance theater: for details,
see L. B. Campbell, *Scenes and Machines on the English Stage,*
1923.

For when the sun the grass hath vexed,
The tawny mowers enter next;
Who seem like Israelites to be
Walking on foot through a green sea.   390
To them the grassy deeps divide,
And crowd a lane to either side.°

With whistling scythe and elbow strong,
These massacre the grass along;
While one, unknowing, carves the rail,°   395
Whose yet unfeathered quills her fail.
The edge all bloody from its breast
He draws, and does his stroke detest;
Fearing the flesh untimely mowed°
To him a fate as black forebode.   400

But bloody Thestylis, that waits
To bring the mowing camp° their cates,°
Greedy as kites has trussed it up,
And forthwith means on it to sup;
When on another quick° she lights,   405
And cries, "He called us Israelites;°
But now, to make his saying true,
Rails rain for quails, for manna dew."°

Unhappy birds! what does it boot
To build below the grasses' root,   410
When lowness is unsafe as height,
And chance o'ertakes what scapeth spite?
And now your orphan parents' call
Sounds your untimely funeral.
Death-trumpets creak in such a note,   415
And 'tis the sourdine° in their throat.

---

392 **crowd . . . side** crowd to either side to form a lane.   395 **rail**
corncrake.   399 **untimely mowed** Cf. *Damon the Mower*, line 88.
402 **mowing camp** As the mowers are represented as soldiers,
Thestylis is a camp-follower.   402 **cates** food.   405 **quick** alive.
406 **He . . . Israelites** "He" is the poet (l. 389).   408 **quails . . .
dew** Exodus xvi, 13–14.   416 **sourdine** a hoarse low trumpet; or,
a mute producing this effect.

Or sooner hatch or° higher build!
The mower now commands the field,
In whose new traverse° seemeth wrought
420 A camp of battle newly fought:
Where, as the meads with hay, the plain
Lies quilted o'er with bodies slain;
The women that with forks it fling,
Do represent the pillaging.

425 And now the careless victors play,
Dancing the triumphs of the hay;°
Where every mower's wholesome heat
Smells like an Alexander's sweat,°
Their females fragrant as the mead
430 Which they in fairy circles° tread:
When at their dance's end they kiss,
Their new-made hay not sweeter is.

When after this 'tis piled in cocks,
Like a calm sea it shows the rocks;
435 We wond'ring in the river near
How boats among them safely steer.
Or, like the desert Memphis° sand,
Short pyramids of hay do stand.
And such the Roman camps° do rise
440 In hills for soldiers' obsequies.

This scene again withdrawing° brings
A new and empty face of things;
A leveled space, as smooth and plain
As cloths° for Lely° stretched to stain.
445 The world when first created sure

417 **or** either.   419 **traverse** passage cut through the field.   426 **hay**
country dance (with a pun).   428 **Alexander's sweat** According
to Plutarch, this had a "a passing delightful savor."   430 **fairy circles**
the effect of mycelium. See *Damon the Mower*, line 64.
437 **Memphis** Egyptian city near the Pyramids.   439 **Roman camps**
the tumuli, now known to be of ancient British origin.   441 **scene
. . . withdrawing** continuing the theatrical figure of line 385.
444 **cloths** canvases.   444 **Lely** Sir Peter Lely, the celebrated Dutch
portrait painter who came to England in 1641. (In *1681* it is spelled
Lilly, which misled some editors.)

Was such a table rase° and pure;
Or rather such is the *toril*°
Ere the bulls enter at Madril.°

For to this naked equal flat,
Which Levellers° take pattern at,°   *450*
The villagers in common° chase
Their cattle, which it closer rase;
And what below the scythe increased°
Is pinched yet nearer by the beast.
Such, in the painted world, appeared   *455*
Davenant with th' Universal Herd.°

They seem within the polished grass
A landskip drawn in looking glass;°
And shrunk in the huge pasture show
As spots, so shaped, on faces do.   *460*
Such fleas, ere they approach the eye,
In multiplying glasses lie;°
They feed so wide, so slowly move,
As constellations do above.

Then to conclude these pleasant Acts,   *465*
Denton° sets ope' its cataracts;
And makes the meadow truly be
(What it but seemed before) a sea.
For, jealous of its Lord's long stay,

446 **table rase** *tabula rasa*.   447 **toril** a reminiscence of Marvell's
visit to Spain; but by "toril" he means "bull-ring" and not the
bulls' enclosure, which is the modern sense.   448 **Madril** Madrid.
450 **Levellers** egalitarian political party of the period, favoring the
leveling out of differences in rank, parliamentary representation, etc.
450 **take pattern at** use as a model.   451 **in common** Not only is
the meadow level, it is also a common for grazing, which strength-
ens its use as a model to levellers.   453 **increased** grew.
456 **Davenant . . . Herd** Davenant, a contemporary of Marvell's,
describes in his admired experimental epic, the unfinished *Gondi-
bert*, a painting of the Six Days of Creation. On the sixth day,
"an universal Herd appears." The reference carries on the compari-
son with the new-created world begun in lines 445–46.   458 **land-
skip . . . glass** a landscape shown in a painting as reflected in a
looking glass and thus reduced in size.   461–62 **such . . . lie** so do
fleas appear on the glass before one looks at them through the
microscope.   466 **Denton** the river flowing through these water
meadows.

470 It tries t' invite him thus away.
    The river in itself is drowned
    And isles th' astonished cattle round.

    Let others tell the paradox,
    How eels now bellow in the ox;
475 How horses at their tails do kick,
    Turned as they hang to leeches° quick;
    How boats can over bridges sail,
    And fishes do the stables scale;
    How salmons trespassing are found,
480 And pikes are taken in the pound.

    But I, retiring from the flood,
    Take sanctuary in the wood;
    And, while it lasts, myself embark
    In this yet green, yet growing ark;
485 Where the first carpenter° might best
    Fit timber for his keel have pressed;°
    And where all creatures might have shares,
    Although in armies, not in pairs.

    The double wood of ancient stocks
490 Linked in, so thick an union° locks,
    It like two pedigrees° appears,
    On one hand Fairfax, th' other Veres;
    Of whom though many fell in war,°
    Yet more to heaven shooting are:
495 And, as they Nature's cradle decked,
    Will in green age her hearse expect.

    When first the eye this forest sees
    It seems indeed as wood not trees;
    As if their neighborhood° so old
500 To one great trunk them all did mold.

---

476 **leeches** the superstition that horsehairs in water turned into
eels or leeches.   485 **first carpenter** Noah.   486 **pressed** comman-
deered.   490 **union** As Margoliouth suggests, this noun is the sub-
ject of the sentence—"the two woods are joined at one point just
as the Vere and Fairfax pedigrees are joined."   491 **pedigrees**
genealogical trees.   493 **in war** They were cut down to meet a
wartime demand for timber.   499 **neighborhood** proximity.

There the huge bulk takes place, as meant
To thrust up a fifth° element;
And stretches still so closely wedged
As if the night within were hedged.

Dark all without it knits; within   *505*
It opens passable and thin;
And in as loose an order grows
As the Corinthian° porticoes.
The arching boughs unite between
The columns of the temple green;   *510*
And underneath the wingèd choirs
Echo about their tunèd fires.°

The nightingale does here make choice
To sing the trials of her voice.
Low shrubs she sits in, and adorns   *515*
With music high the squatted thorns.
But highest oaks stoop down to hear,
And list'ning elders prick the ear.
The thorn, lest it should hurt her, draws
Within the skin its shrunken claws.   *520*

But I have for my music found
A sadder, yet more pleasing sound:
The stock doves, whose fair necks are graced
With nuptial rings, their ensigns chaste;
Yet always, for some cause unknown,   *525*
Sad pair, unto the elms they moan.°
O why should such a couple mourn,
That in so equal flames do burn!

Then as I careless on the bed
Of gelid strawberries do tread,   *530*

---

502 **fifth** of different substance from the existing four: earth, water,
air, fire.   505–12 **Dark . . . fires** This is part of Marvell's consider-
able debt to Benlowes. See M. S. Røstvig, *The Happy Man* (Oslo,
1954), pp. 247–48.   508 **Corinthian** the most ornate of the Greek
architectural orders; but also associated with lightness and laxity
(hence "loose" in l. 507).   526 **unto . . . moan** imitated from
Virgil's *nec gemere aeria cessabit turtur ab ulmo, Eclogues* I, line 58.

And through the hazels thick espy
The hatching throstle's shining eye,
The heron from the ash's top
The eldest of its young lets drop,
535 As if it, stork-like,° did pretend
That tribute to its Lord to send.

But most the hewel's° wonders are,
Who here has the *holt-felster's*° care.
He walks still upright from the root,
540 Meas'ring the timber with his foot;
And all the way, to keep it clean,
Doth from the bark the wood-moths glean.
He, with his beak, examines well
Which fit to stand and which to fell.

545 The good he numbers up, and hacks;
As if he marked them with the ax.
But where he, tinkling with his beak,
Does find the hollow oak to speak,
That for his building he designs,
550 And through the tainted side he mines.
Who could have thought the tallest oak
Should fall by such a feeble stroke!

Nor would it, had the tree not fed
A traitor worm, within it bred.
555 (As first our flesh corrupt within
Tempts impotent and bashful sin.)
And yet that worm triumphs not long,
But serves to feed the hewel's young;
While the oak seems to fall content,
560 Viewing the treason's punishment.

Thus I, easy philosopher,
Among the birds and trees confer;
And little now to make me wants,
Or of the fowls or of the plants.

---

535 **stork-like** The stork was held to leave behind one of its young
as a tribute to the owner; the heron is imagined as dropping one
young bird in similar tribute.   537 **hewel** green woodpecker.
538 **holt-felster's** woodcutter's.

Give me but wings as they, and I   565
Straight floating on the air shall fly:
Or turn me but, and you shall see
I was but an inverted tree.°

Already I begin to call
In their most learned original,   570
And where I language want, my signs
The bird upon the bough divines;
And more attentive there doth sit
Than if she were with lime twigs knit.
No leaf does tremble in the wind   575
Which I returning cannot find.

Out of these scattered Sibyl's leaves°
Strange prophecies my fancy weaves;
And in one history consumes,
Like Mexique paintings, all the plumes.°   580
What Rome, Greece, Palestine, ere said
I in this light mosaic° read.
Thrice happy he who, not mistook,
Hath read in Nature's mystic book.

And see how chance's better wit   585
Could with a masque° my studies hit!
The oak-leaves me embroider all,
Between which caterpillars crawl;
And ivy, with familiar trails,
Me licks, and clasps, and curls, and hales.   590

---

568 **inverted tree** "Man is like an inverted tree" is a commonplace,
explored in historical depth by A. B. Chambers (*Studies in the
Renaissance*, 8 [1961], 291–99, where it is traced back to Aristotle
and even to Plato [*Timaeus*, 90 A]—the same work, 91 E, may
be the original of ll. 565–66). A famous example is Swift, *Medita-
tion on a Broomstick*. There is a comic and indecent application in
Rabelais, III. ix.   577 **Sibyl's leaves** palm leaves from which the
Romans foretold the future.   580 **Mexique . . . plumes** pictures
made by sticking feathers together.   582 **mosaic** image assembled
from various (natural) materials; but also with a reference to the
"Mosaic" books; of the two books of God, the Bible and Nature,
Nature is the "lighter."   586 **masque** an allegorical garb, as if for
some masque-like entertainment.

Under this antic cope° I move
Like some great prelate° of the grove.

Then, languishing with ease, I toss
On pallets swoln of velvet moss;
595 While the wind, cooling through the boughs,
Flatters with air my panting brows.
Thanks for my rest, ye mossy banks,
And unto you, cool Zephyrs, thanks,
Who, as my hair, my thoughts too shed,°
600 And winnow from the chaff my head.

How safe, methinks, and strong, behind
These trees have I encamped my mind;
Where Beauty, aiming at the heart,
Bends in some tree its useless dart;
605 And where the world no certain shot
Can make, or me it toucheth not.
But I on it securely play,
And gall its horsemen all the day.

Bind me ye woodbines in your twines,
610 Curl me about ye gadding vines,°
And, Oh, so close your circles lace,
That I may never leave this place.
But, lest your fetters prove too weak,
Ere I your silken bondage break,
615 Do you, O brambles, chain me too,
And courteous briars, nail me through.

Here in the morning tie my chain,
Where the two woods have made a lane;
While, like a guard on either side,
620 The trees before their Lord divide;
This, like a long and equal thread,
Betwixt two labyrinths does lead.
But, where the floods did lately drown,
There at the evening stake me down.

---

591 **cope** outer vestment (ecclesiastical).   592 **prelate** also developed
from the Latin of Benlowes—see Røstvig, p. 248.   599 **shed** sepa-
rate, part.   610 **gadding vines** a reminiscence of *Lycidas*, line 40,
"the gadding vine."

ségの

For now the waves are fall'n and dried,   625
And now the meadows fresher dyed;
Whose grass, with moister color dashed,
Seems as green silks but newly washed.
No serpent new nor crocodile
Remains behind our little Nile;°   630
Unless itself° you will mistake,
Among these meads the only snake.

See in what wanton harmless folds
It everywhere the meadow holds;
And its yet muddy back doth lick,   635
Till as a crystal mirror slick;
Where all things gaze themselves, and doubt
If they be in it or without.
And for his shade which therein shines,
Narcissus-like,° the sun too pines.   640

Oh what a pleasure 'tis to hedge
My temples here with heavy sedge;
Abandoning my lazy side,
Stretched as a bank unto the tide;
Or to suspend my sliding foot   645
On th' osier's underminèd root,
And in its branches tough to hang,
While at my lines the fishes twang!

But now away my hooks, my quills,
And angles, idle utensils.   650
The young Maria° walks tonight;
Hide, trifling youth, thy pleasures slight.
'Twere shame that such judicious eyes
Should with such toys a man surprise;
She, that already is the law   655
Of all her sex, her age's awe.

629-30 **No . . . Nile** referring to the belief that the Nile floods
begat serpents and crocodiles from the mud.   631 **itself** the river.
640 **Narcissus-like** Narcissus was in love with his own reflection
in a pool.   651 **Maria** Mary Fairfax, to whom the poet was tutor.

See how loose Nature, in respect
To her, itself doth recollect;
And everything so whisht° and fine,
660   Starts forthwith to its *bonne mine*.°
The sun himself, of her aware,
Seems to descend with greater care;
And lest she see him go to bed
In blushing clouds conceals his head.

665   So when the shadows laid asleep
From underneath these banks do creep,
And on the river as it flows
With ebon shuts° begin to close;
The modest halcyon° comes in sight,
670   Flying betwixt the day and night;
And such an horror calm and dumb,
Admiring Nature does benumb.

The viscous air, wheresoe'r she° fly,
Follows and sucks her azure dye;
675   The jellying stream compacts below,
If it might fix her shadow so,
The stupid° fishes hang, as plain
As flies in crystal overta'en;
And men the silent scene assist,°
680   Charmed with the sapphire-wingèd mist.°

Maria such, and so doth hush
The world,° and through the evening rush.
No new-born comet such a train

---

659 **whisht** hushed.   660 **bonne mine** good appearance—puts on its
best behavior (*bonne* is disyllabic).   668 **ebon shuts** ebony (black)
shutters.   669 **halcyon** This bird produces absolute calm. See *The
Gallery*, line 35, though here the bird is the kingfisher. Virgil
(*Georgics* III.335 ff) describes its appearance in the calm of evening.
673 **she** the halcyon.   677 **stupid** stupefied.   679 **assist** attend, are
present at.   680 **sapphire-wingèd mist** the kingfisher in flight.
681–82 **Maria . . . world** The influence of a lady over a landscape,
especially an evening landscape, is a poetic theme discussed by
Leishman, pp. 81 ff; and Scoular, p. 147 (with parallel from Théo-
phile de Viau) and pp. 172 ff.

Draws through the sky, nor star new-slain.°
For straight those giddy rockets fail,   685
Which from the putrid earth exhale,
But by her flames, in Heaven tried,
Nature is wholly vitrified.°

'Tis she that to these gardens gave
That wondrous beauty which they have;   690
She straightness on the woods bestows;
To her the meadow sweetness owes;
Nothing could make the river be
So crystal-pure but only she;
She yet more pure, sweet, straight, and fair,   695
Than gardens, woods, meads, rivers are.

Therefore what first she on them spent,
They gratefully again present:
The meadow, carpets where to tread;
The garden, flowers to crown her head;   700
And for a glass, the limpid brook,
Where she may all her beauties look;
But, since she would not have them seen,
The wood about her draws a screen.

For she, to higher beauties raised,   705
Disdains to be for lesser praised.
She counts her beauty to converse
In all the languages as hers;
Nor yet in those herself employs
But for the wisdom, not the noise;   710
Nor yet that wisdom would affect,
But as 'tis Heaven's dialect.

Blest nymph! that couldst so soon prevent
Those trains° by youth against thee meant:
Tears (wat'ry shot that pierce the mind),   715
And sighs (Love's cannon charged with wind),
True praise (that breaks through all defense),

684 **star new-slain** a meteor, thought to be "exhaled" from the
earth (l. 686).   688 **vitrified** as in the incorruptible crystalline
sphere of the fixed stars.   714 **trains** plots, stratagems.

And feigned complying innocence;
But knowing where this ambush lay,
720 She scaped the safe, but roughest way.

This 'tis to have been from the first
In a domestic heaven nursed,
Under the discipline severe
Of Fairfax, and the starry Vere;
725 Where not one object can come nigh
But pure, and spotless on the eye;
And goodness doth itself entail
On females, if there want a male.

Go now, fond sex, that on your face
730 Do all your useless study place,
Nor once at vice your brows dare knit
Lest the smooth forehead wrinkled sit;
Yet your own face shall at you grin,°
Thorough the black-bag° of your skin;
735 When knowledge only could have filled
And virtue all those furrows tilled.

Hence she with graces more divine
Supplies beyond her sex the line;
And, like a sprig of mistletoe,
740 On the Fairfacian oak doth grow;
Whence, for some universal good,
The priest shall cut the sacred bud;
While her glad parents most rejoice,
And make their destiny their choice.°

745 Meantime ye fields, springs, bushes, flowers,
Where yet she leads her studious hours
(Till fate her worthily translates,
And find a Fairfax for our Thwaites),
Employ the means you have by her,
750 And in your kind yourselves prefer;
That, as all virgins she precedes,
So you all woods, streams, gardens, meads.

733 **grin** grimace.   734 **black-bag** mask.   744 **choice** Mary Fairfax
later married the profligate Duke of Buckingham, and so was in-
volved in one of the greatest scandals of the time.

For you Thessalian Tempe's° seat
Shall now be scorned as obsolete;
Aranjuez,° as less, disdained;   *755*
The Bel-Retiro° as constrained;
But name not the Idalian Grove,°
For 'twas the seat of wanton love;
Much less the dead's Elysian Fields—
Yet nor to them your beauty yields.   *760*

'Tis not, what once it was, the world,°
But a rude heap together hurled;
All negligently overthrown,
Gulfs, deserts, precipices, stone.
Your lesser world contains the same,   *765*
But in more decent order tame;
You Heaven's center, Nature's lap,
And Paradise's only map.

But now the salmon-fishers moist
Their leathern boats begin to hoist;   *770*
And, like Antipodes in shoes,°
Have shod their heads in their canoes.°
How tortoise-like, but not so slow,
These rational amphibii° go!
Let's in; for the dark hemisphere   *775*
Does now like one of them° appear.

---

753 **Thessalian Tempe** the Vale of Tempe in Thessaly, a famous ancient "paradise." 755 **Aranjuez** Spanish royal gardens on the Tagus south of Madrid. 756 **Bel-Retiro** Buen Retiro, another royal residence near Madrid. 757 **Idalian Grove** the garden of Venus. 761 **'Tis . . . world** referring to the disorder of a fallen world, to be compared with the order and balance of the microcosm, or little world, of Mary Fairfax, which reflects the state of the world before paradise was lost. 771 **Antipodes in shoes** those who dwell directly opposite us on the globe (their feet pointing to our feet). 772 **shod . . . canoes** coracles ("leathern boats") were so carried. 774 **rational amphibii** Amphibii are animals at home in and out of water; the salmon-fishers, men being "rational animals," are rational amphibii. 776 **like . . . them** in being covered by a hemisphere of darkness like the boat on the salmon-fisher's head.

FLECKNO, AN ENGLISH PRIEST AT ROME°

Obliged by frequent visits of this man,
Whom as priest, poet, and musician,
I for some branch of Melchizedek° took
(Though he derives himself from "my Lord
      Brooke"),°
5 I sought his lodging; which is at the sign
Of the sad Pelican;° subject divine
For poetry. There three staircases high,
Which signifies his triple property,°
I found at last a chamber, as 'twas said,
10 But seemed a coffin set on the stairs' head—
Not higher than sev'n, nor larger than three feet;
Only there was nor seeling, nor a sheet,°
Save that th' ingenious door did as you come
Turn in, and show° to wainscot half the room.

---

0 **Fleckno . . . Rome** Marvell traveled on the Grand Tour, presumably as a tutor, and must have been in Rome sometime between 1645 and 1647, the dates of Flecknoe's residence there. Richard Flecknoe was an English Roman Catholic priest later satirized as the reigning prince of Dullness in Dryden's *Mac Flecknoe.* Marvell's ribald account of their meeting is in the manner of Horatian satire as imitated by Donne. The poem may well have been written soon after the meeting, but remained unpublished till *1681.* 3 **Melchizedek** king, priest and prophet, an Old Testament type of Christ (Gen. xiv. 18). 4 **Lord Brooke** It is not known whether Flecknoe was entitled to claim this connection with Fulke Greville, though he dedicated a book to a lady of the family. 6 **Pelican** a common inn sign; in devotional poetry an emblem of Christ. 8 **triple property** another reference to the joke about Melchizedek. 12 **seeling . . . sheet** "punning on the properties of the coffin and of the room. *Seeling* can mean wall-hangings; black hangings were used at funerals . . . and it means a wainscot. *Sheet* stands for a bed-sheet and a winding-sheet" (Margoliouth). 14 **show** appear.

Yet of his state no man could have complained,   *15*
There being no bed where he entertained:
And though within one cell so narrow pent,
He'd *stanzas*° for a whole *appartement.*°
   Straight without further information,°
In hideous verse, he, and a dismal tone,   *20*
Begins to exorcise, as if I were
Possessed; and sure the devil brought me there.
But I, who now imagined myself brought
To my last trial, in a serious thought
Calmed the disorders of my youthful breast,   *25*
And to my martyrdom preparèd rest.
Only this frail ambition did remain
(The last distemper of the sober brain)°
That there had been some present to assure
The future ages how I did endure;   *30*
And how I, silent, turned my burning ear
Towards the verse; and when that could not hear,
Held him the other; and unchangèd yet,
Asked still for more, and prayed him to repeat:
Till the tyrant, weary to persecute,   *35*
Left off, and tried t' allure me with his lute.
   Now as two instruments, to the same key
Being tuned by art, if the one touchèd be
The other opposite as soon replies,
Moved by the air and hidden sympathies;   *40*
So while he with his gouty fingers crawls
Over the lute, his murmuring belly calls,
Whose hungry guts to the same straitness° twined
In echo to the trembling strings repined.
   I, that perceived now what his music meant,   *45*
Asked civilly if he had eat this Lent.
He answered yes; with such, and such an one.
For he has this of gen'rous, that alone
He never feeds; save only when he tries
With gristly tongue to dart the passing flies.   *50*

---

18 **stanzas** rooms (Italian); punning on the English meaning.
appartement (four syllables).   19 **information** (five syllables).
28 **last . . . brain** a reminiscence of *Lycidas* line 71.   43 **straitness**
tension.

I asked if he eat flesh. And he, that was
So hungry that though ready to say Mass
Would break his fast before, said he was sick,
And th' ordinance° was only politic.
55 Nor was I longer to invite him scant—
Happy at once to make him Protestant
And silent. Nothing now dinner° stayed
But till he had himself a body made.
I mean till he were dressed; for else so thin
60 He stands, as if he only fed had been
With consecrated wafers; and the Host
Hath sure more flesh and blood than he can boast.
This *basso relievo*° of a man,
Who as a camel tall, yet easily can
65 The needle's eye thread without any stitch,°
(His only'impossible is to be rich),°
Lest his too subtle body, growing rare,
Should leave his soul to wander in the air,
He therefore circumscribes himself in rhymes;
70 And swaddled in's own papers seven times,
Wears a close jacket of poetic buff,
With which he doth his third dimension stuff.
Thus armèd underneath, he over all
Does make a primitive *sotana*° fall;
75 And above that yet casts an antic cloak,
Worn at the first Council of Antioch;°
Which by the Jews long hid, and disesteemed,
He heard of by tradition,° and redeemed.
But were he not in this black habit decked,
80 This half-transparent man would soon reflect

---

54 **th' ordinance** against eating meat in Lent.   57 **dinner** The Bod-
leian copy has "our dinner."   63 **basso relievo** bas-relief.   65 **stitch**
pun on the senses of physical pain and sewing.   66 **rich** which is
what makes it as difficult to enter heaven as for a camel to thread
the eye of a needle (Mark x.25, Luke xviii. 25).   74 **sotana** cassock,
soutane.   75 **antic** ancient; crazy.   76 **first . . . Antioch** A.D. 264.
78 **tradition** The authority of unwritten tradition, held by Roman
Catholics to be equal to that of the Scriptures, was an important
difference between Catholic and Protestant; it underlies this joke.

Each color that he passed by, and be seen,
As the chameleon, yellow, blue, or green,
    He dressed, and ready to disfurnish° now
His chamber, whose compactness did allow
No empty place for complimenting doubt,   *85*
But who came last is forced first to go out;
I met one on the stairs who made me stand,
Stopping the passage, and did him demand.
I answered, "He is here, Sir; but you see
You cannot pass to him but thorough° me."   *90*
He thought himself affronted, and replied,
"I whom the Palace never has denied
Will make the way here." I said, "Sir, you'll do
Me a great favor, for I seek to go."
He gath'ring fury still made sign to draw;   *95*
But himself there closèd in a scabbard saw
As narrow as his sword's; and I, that was
Delightful,° said, "There can no body pass
Except by penetration° hither, where
Two make a crowd, nor can three° persons here   *100*
Consist but in one substance."° Then, to fit
Our peace, the priest said I too had some wit:
To prove't, I said, "The place doth us invite
By° its own narrowness, Sir, to unite."
He asked me pardon; and to make me way   *105*
Went down, as I him followed to obey.
But the propitiatory priest had straight
Obliged us, when below, to celebrate
Together our atonement; so increased
Betwixt us two the dinner to a feast.   *110*
    Let it suffice that we could eat in peace,
And that both poems did and quarrels cease

---

83 **disfurnish** i.e., of its occupants (the only furniture). 90 **thorough**
through. 98 **Delightful** delighted. 99 **penetration** the occupation
of the same space by two bodies at the same time (cf. *Horatian Ode*,
1. 42). 100 **Two . . . three** "When two or three are gathered to-
gether in Thy name . . ." *Book of Common Prayer*, "A Prayer of
St. Chrysostom." 101 **in one substance** like the Trinity. 104 **By**
Bodleian MS; *But* in *1681*.

During the table; though my new-made friend
Did, as he threatened, ere 'twere long intend
115 To be both witty'and valiant. I, loath,
Said 'twas too late, he was already both.
    But now, alas, my first tormentor came,
Who satisfied with eating, but not tame,
Turns to recite; though judges most severe
120 After th' assize's dinner mild appear,
And on full stomach do condemn but few,
Yet he more strict my sentence doth renew;
And draws out of the black box of his breast
Ten quire of paper in which he was dressed.
125 Yet that which was a greater cruelty
Than Nero's poem,° he calls charity;
And so the Pelican at his door hung
Picks out the tender bosom to its young.°
    Of all his poems there he stands ungirt
130 Save only two foul copies° for his shirt;
Yet these he promises as soon as clean.
But how I loathed to see my neighbor glean
Those papers, which he pillèd° from within
Like white flecks rising from a leper's skin!
135 More odious than those rags which the French youth
At ordinaries° after dinner show'th,
When they compare their chancres and poulains.°
Yet he first kissed them, and after takes pains
To read; and then, because he understood
140 Not one word, thought and swore that they were good.
But all his praises could not now appease
The provoked author, whom it did displease
To hear his verses, by so just a curse
That were ill made condemned to be read worse;
145 And how (impossible) he made yet more
Absurdities in them than were before.

---

126 **Nero's poem** Suetonious, *Nero*, 23, says that when Nero was
singing it was strictly forbidden for anyone to leave, however press-
ing his necessity.   127–28 **Pelican . . . young** The pelican tears open
its breast and feeds its young on its flesh and blood.   130 **foul
copies** working drafts (also the more obvious sense).   133 **pillèd**
peeled.   136 **ordinaries** inns.   137 **chancres . . . poulains** syphilitic
sores.

For he his untuned voice did fall or raise
As a deaf man upon a viol plays,
Making the half points and the periods run
Confuseder than the atoms in the sun.   *150*
Thereat the poet swelled, with anger full,
And roared out, like Perillus° in's own bull,
"Sir, you read false." "That any one but you
Should know the contrary." Whereat I, now
Made mediator, in my room, said, "Why?   *155*
To say that you read false, Sir, is no lies."°
Thereat the waxen youth relented straight;
But saw with sad despair that 'twas too late.
For the disdainful poet was retired
Home, his most furious satire to have fired   *160*
Against the rebel; who, at this struck dead,
Wept bitterly as disinherited.
Who should commend his mistress now? Or who
Praise him? both difficult indeed to do
With truth. I counseled him to go in time,   *165*
Ere the fierce poet's anger turned to rhyme.
        He hasted; and I, finding myself free,
As one 'scaped strangely from captivity,
Have made the chance be painted; and go now
To hang it in Saint Peter's for a vow.   *170*

---

152 **Perillus** He made a bronze bull as an instrument of execution
to the order of the tyrant Phalaris, and was the first to suffer in it.
156 **is no lie** does not give you the lie (require you to challenge
him).

TO HIS NOBLE FRIEND,
MR. RICHARD LOVELACE, UPON HIS POEMS°

Sir,

Our times are much degenerate from those
Which your sweet muse, which your fair fortune chose,
And as complexions alter with the climes,
Our wits have drawn th' infection of our times.
5   That candid age no other way could tell°
To be ingenious, but by speaking well.
Who best could praise, had then the greatest praise,
'Twas more esteemed to give, than wear the bays;
Modest ambition studied only then
10 To honor not herself, but worthy men.
These virtues now are banished out of town;
Our Civil Wars have lost the civic crown.°
He highest builds, who with most art destroys,
And against others' fame his own employs.
15 I see the envious caterpillar sit
On the fair blossom of each growing wit.
    The air's already tainted with the swarms
Of insects which against you rise in arms:
Word-peckers, paper-rats, book-scorpions,
20 Of wit corrupted, the unfashioned sons.°
The barbèd censurers begin to look
Like the grim consistory on thy book;°

0 **To his Noble Friend . . . Poems.** A commendatory poem prefixed
to Lovelace's *Lucasta* (1649). 5 **could tell** knew. 12 **civic crown**
oak-leaf garland bestowed on one who saves a citizen's life in battle.
20 **Of wit . . . sons** born ill-shaped of the corruption of wit, as
insects of rotten matter. 21–22 **censurers . . . book** In June 1643,
Parliament issued an Ordinance against the printing of unlicensed
books and this remained in force (despite *Areopagitica* [1644] and
other protests). *Lucasta* was licensed in 1648. The *consistory* was a
court of presbyters.

And on each line cast a reforming eye,
Severer than the young Presbytery.°
Till when in vain they have thee all perused,   25
You shall for being faultless be accused.
Some reading your *Lucasta,* will allege
You wronged° in her the House's privilege;°
Some that you under sequestration are,
Because you writ when going to the war;°   30
And one the book prohibits, because Kent
Their first petition by the author sent.°
　　　But when the beauteous ladies came to know
That their dear Lovelace was endangered so
(Lovelace that thawed the most congealèd breast,   35
He who loved best and them defended best;
Whose hand so rudely grasps the steely brand,
Whose hand so gently melts the lady's hand),
They all in mutiny though yet undressed
Sallied, and would in his defense contest.   40
And one the loveliest that was yet ere seen,
Thinking that I too of the rout had been,
Mine eyes invaded with a female spite
(She knew what pain 'twould be to lose that sight).
"O no, mistake not," I replied, "for I   45
In your defense, or in his cause would die.
But he, secure of glory and of time
Above their envy, or mine aid doth climb.
Him, valiant'st men, and fairest nymphs approve;
His book in them finds judgment, with you, love."   50

　　　　　　　　　　　　　　　Andr. Marvell

---

24 **young Presbytery** established 1643.   28 **wronged** abused.   28 **the
House's privilege** Parliamentary privilege includes immunity from
action in the courts for what is said in the House.   30 **Because . . .
war** referring to Lovelace's song *Going to the Wars.* The original text
(in *Lancaster*) has *write.*   31–32 **Kent . . . sent** Lovelace was sent to
prison for presenting to the House of Commons (April 1642) a
Kentish petition asking for control of the militia and the use of the
Book of Common Prayer.

AN HORATIAN ODE UPON CROMWELL'S
RETURN FROM IRELAND°

The forward youth that would appear
Must now° forsake his muses dear,
    Nor in the shadows sing
    His numbers languishing.
5 'Tis time to leave the books in dust,
And oil th' unusèd armor's rust:
    Removing from the wall
    The corslet of the hall.
So restless° Cromwell could not cease
10 In the inglorious arts of peace,
    But through advent'rous war
    Urgèd his active star:
And, like the three-forked lightning, first

0 **An Horatian . . . Ireland** This poem was canceled from all extant copies of *1681* except for one, in the British Museum. Thompson republished it in 1776. Cromwell returned from his ferocious reconquest of Ireland in May, 1650, and in the following month undertook the preventive campaign against Scotland, Fairfax having resigned as commander-in-chief because he thought the Scots should not be compelled to war. Cromwell entered Scotland on 22 July, 1650; the poem, presumably, was written between his return and that date. Though the tone and some of the details derive from Horace, as the title suggests, Marvell also remembered and imitated what Lucan had written, in his epic *Pharsalia*, about Julius Caesar and Pompey; the most suggestive study of these debts is R. H. Syfret's "Marvell's *Horatian Ode*," *Review of English Studies*, new series xii (1961), 160–72. The political stance of Marvell, on which these borrowings have some bearing, is a complicated issue, and the reader is referred to the Introduction. **2 now** "in times like these." The opening lines (1–8) are adapted from Lucan, *Pharsalia*, i. 239–43. **9 restless** a trait of Lucan's Caesar. The passage 9–24 imitates Lucan, i. 143–55.

Breaking the clouds where it was nursed,
    Did thorough° his own side°   *15*
      His fiery way divide.
For 'tis all one to courage high,
The emulous or enemy;
    And with such to inclose
      Is more than to oppose.°   *20*
Then burning through the air he went,
And palaces and temples rent;
    And Caesar's° head at last
      Did through his laurels° blast.
'Tis madness to resist or blame   *25*
The force of angry heaven's flame;
    And, if we would speak true,
      Much to the man is due,
Who, from his private gardens, where
He lived reservèd and austere,   *30*
    As if his highest plot
      To plant the bergamot,°
Could by industrious valor climb
To ruin the great work of Time,
    And cast the kingdom old   *35*
      Into another mold;
Though Justice against Fate complain,
And plead the ancient rights° in vain;
    But those do hold or break
      As men are strong or weak.   *40*
Nature that hateth emptiness,
Allows of penetration° less;
    And therefore must make room
      Where greater spirits come.
What field of all the Civil Wars,   *45*

---

15 **thorough** through. (*1681* has *through*.)   15 **side** (1) party (2) "the lightning is conceived as tearing through the side of its own body the cloud" (Margoliouth).   19–20 **with . . . oppose** to pen him in will produce an even more violent reaction than to fight against him.   23 **Caesar** Charles I, beheaded in 1649.   24 **laurels** thought to be proof against lightning.   32 **bergamot** a variety of pear. 38 **ancient rights** See *Tom May's Death*, line 69.   42 **penetration** See note on *Fleckno*, line 99.

Where his were not the deepest scars?
    And Hampton shows what part
    He had of wiser art—
Where, twining subtile° fears with hope,
50 He wove a net of such a scope,
    That Charles himself might chase
    To Carisbrooke's narrow case;°
That thence the *Royal Actor*° borne
The *tragic scaffold* might adorn,
55   While round the armèd bands
    Did clap° their bloody hands.
He nothing common did or mean
Upon that memorable scene;
    But with his keener° eye
60   The ax's edge did try;°
Nor called the gods with vulgar spite
To vindicate his helpless right,
    But bowed his comely head,
    Down as upon a bed.°

47–52 **And . . . case** In 1648 the King, noting the increased hostility of the Army Council, took flight from his palace at Hampton Court to Carisbrooke in the Isle of Wight. He did not receive the expected welcome; the governor treated him as a prisoner. Thus his flight was in part responsible for what happened later, but the contemporary rumor that Cromwell engineered it—which is what Marvell here has in mind—appears to be without foundation. 49 **subtile** finely woven. 52 **case** cage. 53 **Actor** This theatrical figure is sustained in lines 54 (*tragic scaffold*—stage for the acting of tragedies), 56 (*clapping*) and 58 (*scene*). John Carswell (*T.L.S.* August 1, 1952, p. 501) suggests that lines 57–64 constitute a faintly ironic criticism of an actor's performance. Margoliouth points out that one contemporary account of the King's trial was called *Tragicum Theatrum Actorum* . . . 56 **clap** Some said that the soldiers around the scaffold were ordered to clap, with the object of rendering the King's words inaudible. 59 **keener** keener than the ax's edge. Margoliouth mentions that Latin *acies* means both "eyesight" and "blade." "It is recorded by one [eye-witness] that he had never seen the king's eyes brighter than in his last moment, and by another that he more than once inquired about the sharpness of the axe" (C. V. Wedgwood, *Poetry and Politics under the Stuarts*, 1961, pp. 101–02). 60 **try** test. 63–64 **bowed . . . bed** The Venetian Ambassador reported that the executioners had prepared for resistance on the part of the King by arranging to drag his head down by force; but he told them this was unnecessary, and voluntarily placed his head on the block (see Christopher Hill, *Puritanism and Revolution*, 1958, p. 360 n.1).

This was that memorable hour   65
Which first assured the forcèd° power
    So when they did design
    The Capitol's first line,
A bleeding head where they begun
Did fright the architects to run;   70
    And yet in that the state
    Foresaw its happy fate.°

And now the Irish are ashamed
To see themselves in one year° tamed:
    So much one man can do,   75
    That does both act and know.°

They° can affirm his praises best,
And have, though overcome, confessed
    How good he is, how just,
    And fit for highest trust;   80

Nor yet grown stiffer with command
But still in the Republic's hand;
    How fit he is to sway
    That can so well obey.

He to the Commons'° feet presents
A kingdom, for his first year's rents;   85
    And, what he may,° forbears
    His fame to make it theirs;

And has his sword and spoils ungirt,
To lay them at the public's skirt.°   90
    So when the falcon high
    Falls heavy from the sky,
She, having killed, no more does search,

---

66 **forcèd** gained by force. 67–72 **So . . . fate** The story is told
by Pliny, *Natural History*, xxviii.2. 74 **in one year** Cromwell's
Irish campaign lasted from August, 1649 to May, 1650. 76 **act and
know** This commends Cromwell for contemplative and active vir-
tue, resuming the theme of lines 29–37. 77–90 **They . . . skirt** a
reminiscence of Lucan, ix. 192–200 (magnanimity of Pompey).
77 **They** the Irish. As Margoliouth says, Irish testimony in favor of
Cromwell would have been hard to find at the time; or, one might
add, later. 85 **Commons'** Thompson; *Common* in *1681.* 87 **what
he may** so far as he can.

But on the next green bough to perch;
95   Where, when he first does lure,
The falc'ner has her sure.
What may not then our isle presume
While Victory his crest does plume!
What may not others fear
100   If thus he crown each year!
A Caesar he ere long to Gaul,
To Italy an Hannibal,
And to all states not free
Shall climacteric° be.
105 The Pict° no shelter now shall find
Within his party-colored° mind;
But from this valor sad°
Shrink underneath the plaid—
Happy if in the tufted brake
110 The English hunter him mistake,°
Nor lay his hounds in near
The Caledonian deer.
But thou the Wars' and Fortune's son
March indefatigably on,
115   And for the last effect
Still keep thy sword erect:
Besides the force it has to fright
The spirits of the shady night,°
The same arts that did gain
120   A power must it maintain.°

---

104 **climacteric** critical, marking an epoch.   105 **Pict** name of Celtic
tribe inhabiting Scotland; chosen rather than "Scot" for the sake
of the pun in the next line.   106 **party-colored** variously colored:
Latin *pingere, pictum*, to paint. The Scots were generally regarded
as fickle and treacherous.   107 **sad** severe.   110 **mistake** because
of his colored camouflage.   117–18 **force . . . night** usually inter-
preted as referring to the cross-hilt of the sword, but this would
imply that the sword is held hilt upmost, and this sword is "erect."
Its power against the forces of darkness may then derive, as John
M. Wallace suggests, from "a sun-like glitter on the blade" (*P.M.L.A.*
lxxvii (1962) 44).   119–20 **The . . . maintain** a commonplace of
political theory; for references see John M. Wallace, page 43 and
notes 48–54.

TOM MAY'S DEATH°

As one put drunk° into the packet-boat,
Tom May was hurried hence and did not know't;
But was amazed on the Elysian side,
And with an eye uncertain, gazing wide,
Could not determine in what place he was   5
(For whence in Stephen's Alley° trees or grass?)
Nor whence the Pope's Head° nor the Mitre° lay—
Signs by which still he found and lost his way.
At last while doubtfully he all compares,
He saw near hand, as he imagined, Ares.°   10
Such did he seem for corpulence and port,
But 'twas a man much of another sort;
'Twas Ben° that in the dusky laurel shade
Amongst the chorus of old poets laid,
Sounding of ancient heroes, such as were   15
The subject's safety, and the rebel's fear;

0 **Tom May's Death** Thomas May, 1595–1650, man of letters, court poet and translator of Lucan in a version Marvell obviously knew, transferred his allegiance to the Parliamentary cause during the Civil Wars and wrote a history of the Long Parliament. In denouncing May as mercenary, Marvell attacks the Parliamentary Party as well. Since the poem was presumably written a few months after the *Horatian Ode*, it presents a problem to those who hold that work to be primarily an eulogy of Cromwell and strengthens certain ambiguities in the more important poem. 1 **drunk** May died in his sleep, according to Aubrey, "after drinking with his chin tyed with his cap 'being fatt'; suffocated."   6 **Stephen's Alley** May lived in this Westminster street, which had many taverns. 7 **Pope's Head, Mitre** common inn signs.   10 **Ares** perhaps an innkeeper.   13 **Ben** Ben Jonson, famous for his "mountain belly."

But how a double-headed vulture eats
Brutus and Cassius,° the people's cheats.
But seeing May he varied straight his song,
20 Gently to signify that he was wrong.
"Cups more than civil of Emathian wine,
I sing," said he, "and the Pharsalian sign,
Where the historian of the Commonwealth
In his own bowels sheathed the conquering health."°
25 By this May to himself and them was come;
He found he was translated,° and by whom.
Yet then with foot as stumbling as his tongue
Pressed for his place among the learned throng.
But Ben, who knew not neither foe nor friend,°
30 Sworn enemy to all that do pretend,
Rose; more than ever he was seen severe,
Shook his gray locks, and his own bays did tear
At this intrusion. Then with laurel wand,
The awful sign of his supreme command
35 (At whose dread whisk Virgil himself does quake,
And Horace patiently its stroke does take),
As he crowds in he whipped him o'er the pate,
Like Pembroke at the masque,° and then did rate.
    "Far from these blessed shades tread back again,
40 Most servile wit, and mercenary pen,
Polydore, Lucan, Alan, Vandal, Goth,°
Malignant poet and historian both.
Go seek the novice statesmen, and obtrude

18 **Brutus and Cassius** heroes to republicans, but the darkest villains to royalists or imperialists; Dante places them with Judas in the mouths of Satan.   21–24 **Cups . . . health** a parody of the opening lines of May's translation of Lucan, beginning "Wars more than civil on Emathian plains . . . "   26 **translated** by death and by Jonson.   29 **friend** Jonson had addressed May as his "chosen friend" in *Underwoods* xxi.   38 **Pembroke . . . masque** Lord Pembroke, the Lord Chamberlain, broke his staff on May at a court masque in 1634, "not knowing who he was." May was compensated.   41 **Polydore . . . Goth** Polydore Vergil, Italian historian who came to the English court early in the sixteenth century; and three barbarian tribes.

On them some Roman cast similitude;
Tell them of liberty, the stories fine,   45
Until you all grow consuls in your wine;
Or thou dictator of the glass bestow
On him the Cato, this the Cicero°—
Transferring old Rome hither in your talk,
As Bethlem's House did to Loreto walk.°   50
Foul architect that hadst not eye to see
How ill the measures of these states agree;
And who by Rome's example England lay,
Those but to Lucan, do continue May.°   55
But thee nor ignorance nor seeming good
Misled, but malice fixed and understood.
Because some one than thee more worthy° wears
The sacred laurel, hence are all these tears?
Must therefore all the world be set on flame,
Because a gazette writer° missed his aim?   60
And for a tankard-bearing muse must we
As for the basket° Guelphs and Ghibellines be?
When the sword glitters o'er the judges' head,
And fear has coward churchmen silencèd,
Then is the poet's time, 'tis then he draws,   65
And single fights forsaken virtue's cause.
He, when the wheel of empire whirleth back,
And though the world's disjointed axle crack,
Sings still of ancient rights° and better times,
Seeks wretched good, arraigns successful crimes.   70
But thou, base man, first prostituted hast
Our spotless knowledge and the studies chaste,
Apostatizing from our arts and us,

44–48 **On . . . Cicero** May was fond of making parallels between
Parliamentary and Roman history.   50 **Bethlem's . . . walk** the house
of the Virgin miraculously transported to Loreto.   54 **Those . . .**
May May wrote a *Continuation of Lucan's Historicall Poem till the*
death of Julius Caesar.   57 **more worthy** Sir William Davenant
became Poet Laureate in 1637, when May thought he would be
appointed.   60 **gazette writer** cheap journalist. (Pronounce gázette.)
62 **basket** the *borsa* in which the warring Florentine sects of Guelph
and Ghibelline cast their votes.   69 **ancient rights** See *Horatian*
Ode, line 38.

To turn the chronicler to Spartacus.°
75 Yet wast thou taken hence with equal° fate,
Before thou couldst great Charles his death relate;
But what will deeper wound thy little mind,
Hast left surviving Davenant still behind,
Who laughs to see in this thy death renewed,
80 Right Roman poverty and gratitude.
Poor Poet thou, and grateful Senate they,
Who thy last reck'ning did so largely pay,°
And with the public gravity would come,
When thou hadst drunk thy last to lead thee home—
85 If that can be thy home where Spenser lies
And reverend Chaucer—but their dust does rise
Against thee, and expels thee from their side,
As th' eagle's plumes from other birds divide.°
Nor here thy shade must dwell. Return, return,
90 Where sulph'ry Phlegeton° does ever burn.
The Cerberus with all his jaws shall gnash,
Megaera° thee with all her serpents lash.
Thou riveted unto Ixion's wheel°
Shalt break, and the perpetual vulture feel.°
95 'Tis just what torments poets e'er did feign,
Thou first historically shouldst sustain."
        Thus by irrevocable sentence cast,
        May, only Master of these Revels, passed.
        And straight he vanished in a cloud of pitch,
100   Such as unto the Sabbath bears the witch.

---

74 **chronicler to Spartacus** historian of the revolutionary Parliament. Spartacus was the leader of the slaves' revolt against Rome in 73–71 B.C. 75 **equal** just. 82 **thy . . . pay** The Council of State voted £100 for May's burial in Westminster Abbey. 88 **th' eagle's . . . divide** Eagle feathers were supposed to rot those of other birds. 90 **Phlegeton** a river of hell. 92 **Megaera** serpent-haired Fury. 93 **Ixion's wheel** one of the torments of Hades. 94 **perpetual . . . feel** like Prometheus.

TO HIS WORTHY FRIEND DOCTOR WITTY
UPON HIS TRANSLATION OF THE
POPULAR ERRORS°

Sit further, and make room for thine own fame,
Where just desert enrolls thy honored name
The good interpreter. Some in this task
Take off the cypress° veil, but leave a mask,
Changing the Latin, but do more obscure   5
That sense in English which was bright and pure.
So of translators they are authors grown,
For ill translators make the book their own.
Others do strive with words and forcèd phrase
To add such luster, and so many rays,   10
That but to make the vessel shining, they
Much of the precious metal rub away.
He is translation's thief that addeth more,
As much as he that taketh from the store
Of the first author. Here he maketh blots   15
That mends; and added beauties are but spots.°

0 To his Worthy . . . Errors Witty was a schoolmaster and later
a physician in Hull. He translated a Latin work by James Primrose,
another Hull doctor, on common errors and myths about medicine.
Witty's translation was published in 1651, and Marvell's com-
mendatory verses (this poem, and also a set of Latin verses) were
printed therein. They were republished in *1681*. 4 cypress of fine
linen. 4–16 Take . . . spots Margoliouth notices these lines as
"one of the few scraps of Marvell's literally criticism."

       Caelia° whose English doth more richly flow
Than Tagus, purer than dissolvèd snow,
And sweet as are her lips that speak it, she
20 Now learns the tongues of France and Italy;
But she is Caelia still: no other grace
But her own smiles commend that lovely face;
Her native beauty's not Italianated,
Nor her chaste mind into the French translated;
25 Her thoughts are English, though her sparkling wit
With other language doth them fitly fit.
       Translators, learn of her. But stay, I slide
Down into error with the vulgar tide;
Women must not teach here: the Doctor doth
30 Stint them to caudles,° almond-milk,° and broth.
Now I reform, and surely so will all
Whose happy eyes on thy translation fall.
I see the people hast'ning to thy book
Liking themselves the worse the more they look,
35 And so disliking, that they nothing see
Now worth the liking, but thy book and thee.
And (if I judgment have) I censure right;
For something guides my hand that I must write.
You have translation's statutes best fulfilled,
40 That handling neither sully nor would gild.

17 Caelia perhaps Mary Fairfax; see *Upon Appleton House,* lines
707–08. Marvell may have written these lines at Nun Appleton in
the winter of 1650–51.   **30 caudles** gruels.   **30 almond-milk** prepa-
ration of blanched almonds and water, used as an emollient.

THE CHARACTER OF HOLLAND°

Holland, that scarce deserves the name of land,
As but th' off-scouring of the British sand;
And so much earth as was contributed
By English pilots when they heaved the lead;
Or what by th' ocean's slow alluvion° fell,   5
Of shipwrecked cockle and the mussel shell;
This indigested vomit of the sea
Fell to the Dutch by just propriety.
    Glad then, as miners that have found the ore,
They with mad labor fished the land to shore;   10
And dived as desperately for each piece
Of earth, as if't had been of ambergris;
Collecting anxiously small loads of clay,
Less than what building swallows bear away;
Or than those pills which sordid beetles roll,   15
Transfusing into them their dunghill soul.
    How did they rivet, with gigantic piles,
Thorough° the center their new-catchèd miles;
And to the stake a struggling country bound,
Where barking waves still bait the forcèd ground;°   20
Building their wat'ry Babel far more high
To reach the sea, than those to scale the sky.

---

0 **The Character of Holland** The first hundred lines, together with
an eight-line conclusion not by Marvell, were published in 1665.
The whole work appeared in *1681.* Marvell probably wrote it in
1653, after the English victory over the Dutch fleet off Portland
in February, and before the engagement of June 3, in which Deane
was killed. 5 **alluvion** matter deposited by flood or inundation
(*O.E.D.*). 18 **Thorough** through. 19–20 **And . . . ground** the figure
is from bear-baiting.

Yet still his claim the injured ocean laid,
And oft at leap-frog o'er their steeples played:
25 As if on purpose it on land had come
To show them what's their *Mare Liberum*.°
A daily deluge over them does boil;
The earth and water play at *level-coyl;*°
The fish oft times the burgher dispossessed,
30 And sat not as a meat but as a guest;
And oft the Tritons and the sea nymphs saw
Whole shoals of Dutch served up for *cabillau;*°
Or as they over the new level ranged
For pickled herring, pickled *Heeren* changed.
35 Nature, it seemed, ashamed of her mistake,
Would throw their land away at duck and drake.°
Therefore necessity, that first made kings,
Something like government among them brings.
For as with Pygmies who best kill the crane,
40 Among the hungry he that treasures grain,
Among the blind the one-eyed blinkard reigns,
So rules among the drownèd he that drains.
Not who first see the rising sun commands,
But who could first discern the rising lands.
45 Who best could know to pump an earth so leak,°
Him they their Lord and country's Father speak.
To make a bank was a great plot of state;
Invent a shov'l and be a magistrate.
Hence some small *Dyke-grave*° unperceived invades
50 The power, and grows as 'twere a "king of spades":
But for less envy some joint States endures,
Who look like a commission of the sewers.
For these *Half-anders,*° half wet and half dry,
Nor bear strict service, nor pure liberty.

---

26 **Mare Liberum** title of a book by the Dutch lawyer and scholar Grotius claiming the freedom of the seas. The Commonwealth Government claimed the Channel as British and required foreign ships to salute the English flag.   28 **level-coyl** a rough game, one player unseating the other (*lever le cul*).   32 **cabillau** codfish.   36 **duck and drake** skimming flat stones across water.   45 **leak** leaky.   49 **Dyke-grave** officer in charge of sea-walls.   53 **Half-anders** not Hollanders (Whole-anders).

'Tis probable religion after this   55
Came next in order; which they could not miss.
How could the Dutch but be converted, when
Th' Apostles were so many fishermen?
Besides the waters of themselves did rise,
And, as their land, so them did re-baptize: 60
Though herring for their God few voices missed,
And Poor-John° to have been th' Evangelist.
Faith, that could never twins conceive before,
Never so fertile, spawned upon this shore:
More pregnant than their Marg'ret,° that laid down   65
For *Hans-in-Kelder*° of a whole *Hans-town*.°

    Sure when religion did it self embark,
And from the east would westward steer its ark,
It struck, and splitting on this unknown ground,
Each one thence pillaged the first piece he found: 70
Hence Amsterdam, Turk-Christian-Pagan-Jew,
Staple of sects and mint of schism grew;
That bank of conscience, where not one so strange
Opinion but finds credit, and exchange.
In vain for catholics ourselves we bear;   75
The Universal Church is only there.
Nor can civility there want for tillage,
Where wisely for their court they chose a village.°
How fit a title clothes their governors,
Themselves the *Hogs*° as all their subjects *Bores!*°   80

    Let it suffice to give their country fame
That it had one Civilis° called by name,
Some fifteen-hundred and more years ago;
But surely never any that was so.

    See but their mermaids with their tails of fish,   85
Reeking at church over the chafing dish.°

---

62 **Poor-John** dried hake.   65 **Marg'ret** legendary Dutch countess who had 365 children at a birth.   66 **Hans-in-Kelder** child in the womb. **Hans-town** member of the Hanseatic League of cities. 78 **village** the Hague, which was denied the status of town till the Napoleonic Wars.   80 **Hogs** *Hoog-mogoden* "high and mighty" was the style in which the States-General were addressed.   80 **Bores** boors (with a pun on "boars").   82 **Civilis** chief of the Batavi in the fight against Rome, A.D. 69.   86 **chafing dish** The Dutch carried stoves to church.

A vestal turf enshrined in earthen ware
Fumes through the loop-holes of a wooden square.
Each to the temple with these altars tend,
90 But still does place it at her western end:
While the fat steam of female sacrifice
Fills the priest's nostrils and puts out his eyes.
　　　Or what a spectacle the skipper gross,
A water-Hercules *butter-Coloss,*°
95 Tunned up with all their sev'ral towns of *Beer;*°
When stagg'ring upon some land, *snick and sneer,*°
They try, like statuaries, if they can,
Cut out each other's Athos° to a man:
And carve in their large bodies, where they please,
100 The arms of the United Provinces.
　　　But when such amity at home is showed,
What then are their confederacies abroad?
Let this one court'sy witness all the rest:
When their whole navy they together pressed,
105 Not Christian captives to redeem from bands,
Or intercept the western golden sands—
No, but all ancient rights and leagues must vail,°
Rather than to the English strike their sail;
To whom their weather-beaten province owes
110 Itself, whenas some greater vessel tows
A cock-boat tossed with the same wind and fate—
We buoyed so often up their sinking state.
　　　Was this *Jus Belli & Pacis?*° Could this be
Cause why their Burgomaster of the sea°
115 Rammed with gunpowder,° flaming with brand wine,°
Should raging hold his linstock° to the mine,

---

94 **butter-Coloss** Butter-box, nickname for Dutchman.   95 **towns of Beer** place names beginning Beer- or Bier-.   96 **snick and sneer** cut and thrust.   98 **cut . . . Athos** Deinocrates the sculptor wanted to cut Mount Athos into the shape of Alexander. They want to cut each other's formless bulk into human shape.   107 **vail** salute by lowering colors; here, surrender.   113 **Jus Belli & Pacis** Grotius wrote *De iure belli et pacis* (*On the Law of War and Peace*).   114 **Burgomaster of the sea** Admiral Van Tromp.   115 **gunpowder** fortified spirits. **brand wine** brandy.   116 **linstock** forked staff holding a lighted match.

While, with feigned treaties, they invade by stealth
Our sore° new-circumcisèd Commonwealth?
    Yet of his vain attempt no more he sees
Than of case-butter° shot and bullet-cheese;°   *120*
And the torn navy staggered with him home,
While the sea laughed itself into a foam.
'Tis true since that (as fortune kindly° sports),
A wholesome danger drove us to our ports,°
While half their banished keels the tempest tossed, *125*
Half bound at home in prison to the frost:
That ours meantime at leisure might careen,°
In a calm winter, under skies serene;
As the obsequious air and waters rest,
Till the dear halcyon° hatch out all its nest.   *130*
The Commonwealth doth by its losses grow;
And, like its own seas, only ebbs to flow:
Besides that very agitation laves,
And purges out the corruptible° waves.
    And now again our armèd *Bucentore*°   *135*
Doth yearly our sea-nuptials restore.
And now the hydra of seven provinces°
Is strangled by our infant Hercules.
Their tortoise wants° its vainly stretchèd neck;
Their navy all our conquest or our wreck: *140*
Or, what is left, their Carthage, overcome,
Would render fain unto our better Rome.
Unless our Senate, lest their youth disuse,
The war—but who would peace if begged refuse?

---

118 **sore** Gen. xxxiv. 25.   120 **case-butter** canister-shot using butter.
bullet-cheese bullets made of cheese.   123 **kindly** according to her
nature.   124 A . . . **ports** Blake took refuge in port after an en-
gagement with Van Tromp in November 1652.   127 **careen** be
heeled over on their sides for repair.   130 **halcyon** See *Appleton
House*, line 669, and *The Gallery*, line 35. The halcyon was some-
times said to nest at the winter solstice, thus causing a calm.
134 **corruptible** Several officers were discharged after an enquiry
into the action of November, 1652.   135 **Bucentore** the Doge's gal-
ley, center of the ceremony of Venice wedding the sea.   137 **seven
provinces** the United Provinces of the Netherlands.   139 **wants** we
have chopped it off.

145   For now of nothing may our State despair,
        Darling of Heaven, and of men the care,
        Provided that they be what they have been,
        Watchful abroad, and honest still within.
        For while our Neptune doth a trident shake,
        Steeled with those piercing heads, Deane, Monck and
150   Blake,°
        And while Jove governs in the highest sphere,
        Vainly in hell let Pluto domineer.

150 **Deane, Monck and Blake** Deane and Monck were colonels,
appointed generals of the fleet in association with Blake. Deane
was killed June 3, 1653.

from THE FIRST ANNIVERSARY OF THE
GOVERNMENT UNDER O. C.°

Like the vain curlings of the wat'ry maze,
Which in smooth streams a sinking weight docs raise;
So man, declining always, disappears
In the weak circles of increasing years;
And his short tumults of themselves compose,   5
While flowing time above his head does close.
    Cromwell alone with greater vigor runs
(Sun-like) the stages of succeeding suns:

0 **The First . . . O. C.** published as a quarto in 1655 and reprinted
but canceled, in *1681.* Cromwell became Protector in December,
1653. When Marvell wrote the poem he was at Eton, tutor to
Cromwell's protégé William Dutton. J. A. Mazzeo has argued that
Marvell represents Cromwell here as a Davidic king; the concept of
the *regnum Davidicum* had long been associated with European
kingship, e.g. in coronation rituals (*Renaissance and Seventeenth-
Century Studies,* 1964, Cap. IX). John M. Wallace treats the poem
as a "deliberative" one, about Cromwell instituting a new dynasty,
Marvell holding that the choice of king was human, but that anoint-
ment ought to follow; after election, the grace of God. The suc-
cession must be assured against accidents and Fifth Monarchy
machinations ("Andrew Marvell and Cromwell's Kingship, *The
First Anniversary,*" *E.L.H.,* xxx [1963] 209–235). The poem has
seven principal sections, of which the fourth and fifth are here
omitted The fourth describes Cromwell's accident (his coach over-
turned in Hyde Park, September 1654) and the fifth defends Crom-
well against the charges that he exercised arbitrary power. These,
together with the opening 18 lines of the sixth section, make a cut of
152 lines. What remains consists of (1) 1–48, celebration of Crom-
well's monarchic vigor and integrity; (2) 49–116, his building of an
harmonious state; (3) 117–158, delay in arrival of the millennium be-
cause of human folly; (6) 311–324, attack on the Fifth Monarchy
men; (7) 325–402, envy and admiration of foreign princes, and
conclusion.

And still the day which he doth next restore,
10 Is the just wonder of the day before.
Cromwell alone doth with new luster spring,
And shines the jewel in the yearly ring.°
    'Tis he the force of scattered time contracts,
And in one year the work of ages acts.°
15 While heavy monarchs make a wide return,
Longer, and more malignant than Saturn.°
And though they all Platonic years° should reign,
In the same posture would be found again.
Their earthy projects under ground they lay,
20 More slow and brittle than the China clay:°
Well may they strive to leave them to their son,
For one thing never was by one king done.
Yet some° more active, for a frontier town
Took in by proxy, begs a false renown;
25 Another triumphs at the public cost,
And will have won, if he no more have lost;
They fight by others, but in person wrong,
And only are against their subjects strong;
Their other wars seem but a feigned contest,
30 This common enemy° is still oppressed;
If conquerors, on them they turn their might;
If conquerèd, on them they wreak their spite:
They neither build the temple° in their days,
Nor matter for succeeding founders raise;
35 Nor sacred prophecies consult within,
Much less themselves to pérfect them begin;
No other care they bear of things above,
But with astrologers divine, and Jove,

12 **the jewel . . . ring** like the sun in the zodiac.   13–14 **the force . . . acts** Compare the different version in *Horatian Ode*, line 34. 16 **Saturn** which had the longest orbit of the known planets. 17 **Platonic years** A Platonic year is the period required for all the planets to return to their original relative positions; estimated at 36,000 years.   20 **China clay** It was believed that the Chinese made porcelain by burying clay in the ground.   23 **some** some king.   30 **common enemy** the subjects.   33 **temple** David was commanded to leave the building of the Temple to Solomon (1 Chron. xxviii).

To know how long their planet yet reprieves
From the deservèd fate their guilty lives:
Thus (image-like)° an useless time they tell,　　40
And with vain scepter strike the hourly bell;
Nor more contribute to the state of things,
Than wooden heads unto the viol's strings.

　　　While indefatigable Cromwell hies,　　45
And cuts his way still nearer to the skies,
Learning a music in the region clear,
To tune this lower to that higher sphere.°

　　　So when Amphion° did the lute command,
Which the god° gave him, with his gentle hand,　　50
The rougher stones, unto his measure hewed,
Danced up in order from the quarries rude;
This took a lower, that an higher place,
As he the treble altered, or the bass:
No note he struck, but a new story laid,　　55
And the great work ascended while he played.

　　　The list'ning structures he with wonder eyed,
And still new stops to various time applied:
Now through the strings a martial rage he throws,
And joining straight the Theban tower arose;　　60
Then as he strokes them with a touch more sweet,
The flocking marbles in a palace meet;
But, for he most the graver notes did try,
Therefore the temples reared their columns high:
Thus, ere he ceased, his sacred lute creates　　65
Th' harmonious city of the seven° gates.

　　　Such was the wondrous order and consent,
When Cromwell tuned the ruling Instrument;°

41 **image-like** like clock-figures striking the hour on a bell (Margoliouth). 47–48 **Learning . . . sphere** reference to a familiar body of ideas about *musica humana* and its relation to the harmony of the spheres (see, for full treatment, J. Hollander, *The Untuning of the Sky*, 1961). 49 **Amphion** He built the wall at Thebes by making stones move to music; a stock figure in the formal *laudes musicae*. 50 **the god** Hermes. 66 **seven** appropriately, since there were "six notes of music" and the seventh provided what we should call an octave. 68 **Instrument** a pun; Cromwell's Protectorate was instituted by an Instrument of Government in 1653.

While tedious statesmen many years did hack,°
70 Framing a liberty that still went back;
Whose num'rous gorge could swallow in an hour
That island, which the sea cannot devour:
Then our Amphion issues out and sings,
And once he struck, and twice, the pow'rful strings.

75   The Commonwealth then first together came,
And each one entered in the willing frame;
All other matter yields, and may be ruled;
But who the minds of stubborn men can build?
No quarry bears a stone so hardly wrought,
80 Nor with such labor from its center brought;
None to be sunk in the foundation bends,°
Each in the House the highest place contends,
And each the hand that lays him will direct,
And some fall back upon the architect;
85 Yet all composed by his attractive° song,
Into the animated city throng.

    The Commonwealth does through their centers all
Draw the circumf'rence of the public wall;
The crossest spirits here do take their part,
90 Fast'ning the contignation° which they thwart;
And they, whose nature leads them to divide,
Uphold, this one, and that the other side;
But the most equal still sustain the height,
And they as pillars keep the work upright;
95 While the resistance of opposèd minds,
The fabric as with arches stronger binds,
Which on the basis of a Senate free,
Knit by the roof's protecting weight agree.

    When for his foot he thus a place° had found,
100 He hurls e'er since the world about him round;
And in his sev'ral aspects,° like a star,
Here shines in peace, and thither shoots a war:

---

69 **hack** muddle.   81 **bends** consents.   85 **attractive** in the literal
sense; he draws them as Amphion did the stones.   90 **contignation**
a joining together of boards.   99 **a place** Archimedes said that
given a fulcrum he could move the earth.   101 **aspects** astrological
term: planets in varying positions have good or ill aspects toward
the earth.

While by his beams observing princes steer,
And wisely court the influence° they fear.
O would they rather by his pattern won,   105
Kiss the approaching, nor yet angry Son;
And in their numbered footsteps humbly tread
The paths where holy oracles do lead;°
How might they under such a captain raise
The great designs kept for the Latter Days!°   110
But mad with reason (so miscalled) of state,
They know them not, and what they know not, hate.
Hence still they sing Hosanna to the Whore,
And her whom they should massacre, adore:
But Indians° whom they should convert, subdue;   115
Nor teach, but traffic with, or burn the Jew.°

    Unhappy princes, ignorantly bred,
By malice some, by error more misled;
If gracious Heaven to my life give length,
Leisure to time, and to my weakness strength,   120
Then shall I once with graver accents shake
Your regal sloth, and your long slumbers wake:
Like the shrill huntsman that prevents the east,
Winding his horn to kings that chase the beast.

    Till then my muse shall hollo° far behind   125
Angelic Cromwell who outwings the wind;
And in dark nights, and in cold days alone
Pursues the Monster thorough° every throne:
Which shrinking to her Roman den impure,
Gnashes her gory teeth; nor there secure.   130

    Hence oft I think, if in some happy hour
High Grace should meet in one with highest power,
And then a seasonable people still

---

104 **influence** also astrological.   105–8 **O . . . lead** See Psalm ii,
10–12.   110 **Latter Days** Dan. ii. 28, x. 14. These are apocalyptic
lines; many believed in the approaching Fifth Monarchy of the
Saints (Dan. vii. 18), after the destruction of the Great Whore
(Rome) and the Beast.   115 **Indians** As one of the nations, they
should be brought in, not subdued.   116 **Jew** The conversion of
the Jews would precede the Latter Days. Cromwell, in 1656, re-
admitted the Jews to England, to facilitate this development.
125 **hollo** huntsman's cry.   128 **thorough** through.

Should bend to his, as he to Heaven's will,
135 What we might hope, what wonderful effect
From such a wished conjuncture might reflect.
Sure, the mysterious work, where none withstand,
Would forthwith finish under such a hand;
Foreshortened Time its useless course would stay,
140 And soon precipitate the Latest Day.
But a thick cloud about the Morning lies,
And intercepts the beams of mortal eyes,
That 'tis the most which we determine can:
If these the Times, then this must be the Man.
145 And well he therefore does, and well has guessed,
Who in his age has always forward pressed;
And knowing not where Heaven's choice may light,
Girds yet his sword, and ready stands to fight;
But men alas, as if they nothing cared,
150 Look on, all unconcerned, or unprepared;
And stars still fall, and still the Dragon's tail
Swinges the volumes of its horrid flail.
For the great Justice that did first suspend
The world by sin, does by the same extend.
155 Hence that blest Day still counterpoisèd wastes,
The ill delaying, what th' Elected hastes;
Hence landing Nature to new seas is tossed,
158 And good designs still with their authors lost.

* * *

311   Accursèd locusts,° whom your King does spit
Out of the center of th' unbottomed Pit;
Wand'rers, adult'rers, liars, Munser's rest,°
Sorcerers, atheists, Jesuits, possessed;
315 You who the Scriptures and the laws deface
With the same liberty as points° and lace;
O race most hypocritically strict!
Bent to reduce us to the ancient Pict;
Well may you act the Adam and the Eve;°

311 **locusts** Rev. ix, 2, 3, 11; a passage generally associated with
heretics.   313 **Munser's rest** Munser, in Westphalia, was taken in
1534 by the Anabaptists. This means: Anabaptists, etc., left over
from Munster.   316 **points** for fastening hose.   319 **act . . . Eve**
Adamite sects went naked.

Aye, and the Serpent too that did deceive.   320
    But the great Captain, now the danger's o'er,
Makes you for his sake tremble one fit more;
And, to your spite, returning yet alive
Does with himself all that is good revive.
    So when first man did through the morning new   325
See the bright sun his shining race pursue,
All day he followed with unwearied sight,
Pleased with that other world of moving light;
But thought him when he missed his setting beams,
Sunk in the hills, or plunged below the streams.   330
While dismal blacks hung round the universe,
And stars (like tapers) burned upon his hearse;
And owls and ravens with their screeching noise
Did make the fun'rals sadder by their joys:
His weeping eyes the doleful vigils keep,   335
Not knowing yet the night was made for sleep.
Still to the west, where he him lost, he turned,
And with such accents, as despairing, mourned:
"Why did mine eyes once see so bright a ray?
Or why day last no longer than a day?"   340
When straight the sun behind him he descried,
Smiling serenely from the further side.
    So while our star that gives us light and heat,
Seemed now a long and gloomy night to threat,
Up from the other world his flame he darts,   345
And princes, shining through their windows, starts;
Who their suspected councillors refuse,
And credulous ambassadors accuse.
    "Is this," said one, "the nation that we read
Spent with both wars,° under a captain dead?   350
Yet rig a navy while we dress us late;
And ere we dine, raze and rebuild their state.
What oaken forests, and what golden mines!
What mints of men, what union of designs!

---

350 **both wars** the Civil War and the Dutch War.

355 Unless their ships do, as their fowl, proceed
       Of shedding leaves,° that with their ocean breed.
       Theirs are not ships, but rather arks of war,
       And beakèd promontories sailed from far;
       Of floating islands a new hatchèd nest;
360 A fleet of worlds, of other worlds in quest;
       An hideous shoal of wood-leviathans,
       Armed with three tiers of brazen hurricanes;°
       That through the center shoot their thund'ring side
       And sink the earth that does at anchor ride.
365 What refuge to escape them can be found,
       Whose wat'ry leaguers° all the world surround?
       Needs must we all their tributaries be,
       Whose navies hold the sluices of the sea?
       The ocean is the fountain of command,
370 But that once took, we captives are on land.
       And those that have the waters for their share,
       Can quickly leave us neither earth nor air.
       Yet if through these our fears could find a pass;
       Through double oak, and lined with treble brass,
375 That one man still, although but named, alarms
       More than all men, all navies, and all arms.
       Him, all the day, him, in late nights I dread,
       And still his sword seems hanging o'er my head.
       The nation had been ours, but his one soul
380 Moves the great bulk, and animates the whole.
       He secrecy with number hath enchasèd,°
       Courage with age, maturity with haste;
       The valiant's terror, riddle of the wise;
       And still his falchion all our knots° unties.
385 Where did he learn those arts that cost us dear?
       Where below earth, or where above the sphere?

356 **shedding leaves** A kind of goose was thought to be bred from
leaves fallen into water.   362 **brazen hurricanes** bronze cannon.
366 **leaguers** besieging forces.   381 **enchased** worked in together.
384 **our knots** alluding to the Gordian knot: whoever untied it would
be master of the world. Alexander cut it.

He seems a king by long succession born,
And yet the same to be a king does scorn.
Abroad a king he seems, and something more,
At home a subject on the equal floor.   390
O could I once him with our title see,
So should I hope yet he might die as we.
But let them write his praise that love him best.
     Pardon, great Prince, if thus their fear or spite
More than our love and duty do thee right.   395
I yield, nor further will the prize contend;
So that we both alike may miss our end:
While thou thy venerable head dost raise
As far above their malice as my praise,
And as the angel of our commonweal,   400
Troubling the waters, yearly mak'st them heal.°

400–01 **And . . . heal** In John v. 4 an angel troubles the water and
it cures the sick. Cromwell did it by accepting the Protectorate in
December, 1653, and was about to do it again by dissolving Parlia-
ment in January, 1655.

TWO SONGS AT THE MARRIAGE OF THE LORD FAUCONBERG AND THE LADY MARY CROMWELL°

FIRST SONG

Chorus. Endymion. Luna.

Chorus.	Th' astrologer's own eyes° are set,
	And even wolves the sheep forget;
	Only this shepherd, late and soon,
	Upon this hill outwakes the moon.
	Hark how he sings, with sad delight,
	Thorough the clear and silent night.

Endymion.	Cynthia, O Cynthia, turn thine ear,
	Nor scorn Endymion's plaint to hear.
	As we our flocks, so you command
	The fleecy clouds with silver wand.

Cynthia.	If thou a mortal, rather sleep;
	Or if a shepherd, watch thy sheep.

5

10

---

0 **Two Songs . . . Cromwell** Mary Cromwell, third daughter of the Protector, married Lord Fauconberg November 19, 1657 at Hampton Court. These songs probably belong to a musical entertainment devised for the wedding.   1 **eyes** as well as his stars.

Endymion.   The shepherd, since he saw thine
                  eyes,
               And sheep are both thy sacrifice.
               Nor merits he a mortal's name,   *15*
               That burns with an immortal flame.

Cynthia.   I have enough for me to do,
               Ruling the waves that ebb and flow.

Endymion.   Since thou disdain'st not then to
                  share
               On sublunary things thy care;   *20*
               Rather restrain these double seas,
               Mine eyes' incessant deluges.

Cynthia.   My wakeful lamp all night must
                  move,
               Securing their repose above.

Endymion.   If therefore thy resplendent ray   *25*
               Can make a night more bright than
                  day;
               Shine thorough° this obscurer breast,
               With shades of deep despair
                  oppressed.

Chorus.   Courage, Endymion, boldly woo;
               Anchises° was a shepherd too,   *30*
               Yet is her younger sister laid
               Sporting with him in Ida's shade:
                  And Cynthia, though the
                  strongest,
               Seeks but the honor to have held out
                  longest.

---

27 **thorough** through   30 **Anchises** lover of Venus; but here Robert
Rich, who a week earlier had married Cromwell's fourth daughter
Frances.

35 *Endymion.*   Here unto Latmos'° top I climb:
                      How far below thine orb sublime?
                      O why, as well as eyes to see,
                      Have I not arms that reach to thee?

   Cynthia.   'Tis needless then that I refuse,
40   Would you but your own reason
                                use.

   Endymion.   Though I so high may not pretend,
                      It is the same so you descend.

   Cynthia.   These stars would say I do them
                                wrong,
                      Rivals each one for thee too strong.

45 *Endymion.*   The stars are fixed unto their sphere,
                      And cannot, though they would,
                                come near.
                      Less loves set off each other's praise,
                      While stars eclipse by mixing rays.

   Cynthia.   That cave is dark.

   Endymion.   Then none can spy:
50   Or shine thou there and 'tis the sky.

   Chorus.   Joy to Endymion,
                      For he has Cynthia's favor won.
                                And Jove himself approves
                      With his serenest influence their loves.
55   For he did never love to pair
                      His progeny above the air;
                      But to be honest, valiant, wise,
                      Makes mortals matches fit for deities.

---

35 **Latmos** the mountain upon which Endymion and Cynthia con-
sorted.

SECOND SONG

Hobbinol. Phyllis. Tomalin.

Hobbinol.   Phyllis, Tomalin, away:
                     Never such a merry day.
                     For the northern shepherd's son°
                     Has Menalca's daughter won.

Phyllis.   Stay till I some flowers ha' tied   5
                     In a garland for the bride.

Tomalin.   If thou wouldst a garland bring,
                     Phyllis you may wait the spring:
                     They ha' chosen such an hour
                     When *she* is the only flower.   10

Phyllis.   Let's not then at least be seen
                     Without each a sprig of green.

Hobbinol.   Fear not; at Menalca's hall
                     There is bays enough for all.
                     He when young as we did graze,   15
                     But when old he planted bays.

Tomalin.   Here *she* comes; but with a look
                     Far more catching than my hook.
                     'Twas those eyes, I now dare swear,
                     Led our lambs we knew not where.   20

Hobbinol.   Not our lambs' own fleeces are
                     Curled so lovely as her hair:
                     Nor our sheep new washed can be
                     Half so white or sweet as *she*.

Phyllis.   *He* so looks as fit to keep   25
                     Somewhat else than silly sheep.

---

3 **northern shepherd's son** Fauconberg was from Yorkshire, a kins-
man of Fairfax.

Hobbinol.   Come, let's in some carol new
                               Pay to love and them their due.

All.   Joy to that happy pair,
30   Whose hopes united banish our despair.
                               What shepherd could for love
                                        pretend,
               Whilst all the nymphs on Damon's choice
                                        attend?
                               What shepherdess could hope to wed
                               Before Marina's turn were sped?
35   Now lesser beauties may take place,
                               And meaner virtues come in play;
                                        While they,
                                   Looking from high,
                                        Shall grace
40   Our flocks and us with a propitious eye.
                               But what is most, the gentle swain
                               No more shall need of love complain;
                               But virtue shall be beauty's hire,
               And those be equal that have equal fire.
45   Marina yields. Who dares be coy?
               Or who despair, now Damon does enjoy?
                                   Joy to that happy pair,
               Whose hopes united banish our despair.

from A POEM UPON THE DEATH OF O. C.°

Valor, religion, friendship, prudence died
At once with him, and all that's good beside;
And we, death's refuse, nature's dregs, confined
To loathsome life, alas! are left behind.   230
Where we (so once we used) shall now no more,
To fetch day, press about his chamber-door;
From which he issued with that awful state,
It seemed Mars broke through Janus' double gate;°
Yet always tempered with an air so mild,   235
No April suns that e'er so gently smiled;

0 A Poem . . . O. C. Together with *An Horatian Ode* and *The First
Anniversary*, this poem was canceled from *1681*, though not from
the British Museum copy; however, even in that 140 lines are
wanting (185–324). These were provided by Thompson, but occur
also in Bodleian MS. Eng. poet. d.49, which is probably the book
Thompson describes as having come into his hands when he had
finished preparing his edition. Cromwell died September 3, 1658.
Marvell's poem is a long funeral elegy on the general pattern of
such things (see Wallerstein, *Seventeenth-Century Poetic*, 1950) but
it also reveals some of the political tensions experienced by the poet
at this time. The poem opens with a passage remarking that the
last act of Cromwell's tragedy cannot be violent death, since his
enemies are all slain by his valor or disarmed of malice by his
clemency; so his end was appropriate to greatness accompanied by
softness of heart. His love and grief for his daughter Elizabeth
(died August 6, 1658) brought his end, which was presaged by a
portentous storm. The date of his death was appropriate, since
September 3 was the anniversary of both the Battle of Dunbar and
the Battle of Worcester. Cromwell's fame surpasses that of King
Arthur:

    He first put arms into Religion's hand,
    And tim'rous Conscience unto Courage manned;
    The soldier taught that inward mail to wear,
    And fearing God how they should nothing fear.   (179–82)

There follows the passage here printed, beginning with the kind of
hyperbole customary in such poems and most familiar to us from
Donne's *Anniversaries*.   234 **Janus' double gate** the *Ianus geminus*
in the Forum at Rome.

No more shall hear that powerful language charm,
Whose force oft spared the labor of his arm;
No more shall follow where he spent the days
240 In war, in counsel, or in pray'r, and praise;
Whose meanest acts he would himself advance,
As ungirt David° to the Ark did dance.
All, all is gone of ours or his delight
In horses fierce, wild deer, or armor bright;
245 Francisca° fair can nothing now but weep,
Nor with soft notes shall sing his cares asleep.
      I saw him dead. A leaden slumber lies,
And mortal sleep over those wakeful eyes;
Those gentle rays under the lids were fled,
250 Which through his looks that piercing sweetness shed;
That port which so majestic was and strong,
Loose and deprived of vigor, stretched along;
All withered, all discolored, pale and wan—
How much another thing, no more that man?
255 Oh human glory, vain, Oh death, oh wings,
Oh worthless world, oh transitory things!
Yet dwelt that greatness in his shape decayed,
That still though dead, greater than death he laid;
And in his altered face you something feign°
260 That threatens death, he yet will live again.
         Not much unlike the sacred oak, which shoots
To heav'n its branches, and through earth its roots:
Whose spacious boughs are hung with trophies round,
And honored wreaths have oft the victor crowned.
265 When angry Jove darts lightning through the air,
At mortal sins, nor his own plant will spare
(It groans, and bruises all below that stood
So many years the shelter of the wood);
The tree erewhile foreshortened to our view,
270 When fall'n shows taller yet than as it grew.°
         So shall his praise to after times increase,
When truth shall be allowed, and faction cease;

242 **David.** "And David danced before the Lord with all his might"
II Samuel, vi. 14.   245 **Francisca** Cromwell's youngest daughter,
Frances.   259 **feign** imagine.   269-70 **The tree . . . grew** Cf. *Eyes
and Tears*, lines 5-6. Also lines 273-74 following.

And his own shadows with him fall: the eye
Detracts from objects than itself more high;
But when death takes them from that envied seat,°   *275*
Seeing how little, we confess how great.
Thee, many ages hence, in martial verse
Shall th' English soldier, ere he charge, rehearse;
Singing of thee, inflame themselves to fight,
And with the name of Cromwell, armies fright.   *280*
As long as rivers to the seas shall run,
As long as Cynthia° shall relieve the sun,
While stags shall fly unto the forests thick,
While sheep delight the grassy downs to pick,
As long as future time succeeds the past,   *285*
Always thy honor, praise and name, shall last.

    Thou in a pitch° how far beyond the sphere
Of human glory tow'rst, and reigning there
Despoiled of mortal robes, in seas of bliss,
Plunging dost bathe and tread the bright abyss;   *290*
There thy great soul yet once a world does see,
Spacious enough, and pure enough for thee.
How soon thou Moses hast, and Joshua found,
And David, for the sword and harp renowned?
How straight canst to each happy mansion go   *295*
(Far better known above than here below)?
And in those joys dost spend the endless day,
Which in expressing, we ourselves betray.

    For we, since thou art gone, with heavy doom,
Wander like ghosts about thy lovèd tomb;   *300*
And lost in tears, have neither sight nor mind
To guide us upward through this region blind.
Since thou art gone, who best that way could'st teach,
Only our sighs, perhaps, may thither reach.

*   *   *°

---

275 seat This reading (Bodleian MS) is certainly right against *state*
(Thompson).   **282 Cynthia** the moon.   **287 pitch** height (as used
in falconry).   **305** The remaining lines of the poem (305–24) felicitate
Richard Cromwell on his succession to the Protectorate, which was
proclaimed on the day of Cromwell's death. Richard resigned in
May 1659, proving quite unable to steer his father's course between
monarchy and republicanism, or to control the Army.

ON MR. MILTON'S *PARADISE LOST*°

When I beheld the poet blind, yet bold,
In slender book his vast design unfold,
Messiah crowned, God's reconciled decree,
Rebelling Angels, the Forbidden Tree,
5   Heav'n, Hell, Earth, Chaos, all: the argument
Held me a while misdoubting his intent,
That he would ruin (for I saw him strong)
The sacred truths to fable and old song—
So Samson groped the temple's posts in spite,
10   The world o'erwhelming to revenge his sight.
      Yet as I read, soon growing less severe,
I liked his project, the success did fear;
Through that wide field how he his way should find
O'er which lame faith leads understanding blind;
15   Lest he perplexed the things he would explain,
And what was easy he should render vain.
      Or if a work so infinite he spanned,
Jealous I was that some less skillful hand
(Such as disquiet always what is well,
20   And by ill imitating would excel)
Might hence presume the whole Creation's Day
To change in scenes, and show it in a play.°

---

0 **On Mr. Milton's Paradise Lost** These verses, signed A.M., were
prefixed to the second edition of *Paradise Lost* (1674) and reprinted
in *1681*. Marvell is known to have supported Milton at the time
of his greatest danger of the Restoration, and he also defended
him in the second part of *The Rehearsal Transpros'd* (1673).
18–22 **less skillful . . . play** Dryden asked and got Milton's per-
mission to adapt *Paradise Lost* for the stage. The result was an
"opera," called *The State of Innocence*, published 1677, and proba-
bly never performed. Marvell obviously disliked Dryden, partly no
doubt because he changed sides at the Restoration, and Dryden
retaliated in the preface to *Religio Laici* (1682).

Pardon me, Mighty Poet, nor despise
My causeless, yet not impious, surmise.
But I am now convinced, and none will dare   25
Within thy labors to pretend a share.
Thou hast not missed one thought that could be fit,
And all that was improper dost omit:
So that no room is here for writers left,
But to detect their ignorance or theft.   30
        That majesty which through thy work does reign
Draws the devout, deterring the profane;
And things divine thou treatst of in such state
As them preserves, and thee, inviolate.
At once delight and horror on us seize,   35
Thou singst with so much gravity and ease;
And above human flight dost soar aloft,
With plume so strong, so equal, and so soft.
The bird named from that Paradise° you sing
So never flags, but always keeps on wing.   40
        Where couldst thou words of such a compass find?
Whence furnish such a vast expense of mind?
Just Heav'n thee, like Tiresias° to requite,
Rewards with prophecy thy loss of sight.
        Well mightst thou scorn thy readers to allure   45
With tinkling rhyme,° of thy own sense secure;
While the *Town-Bayes*° writes all the while and spells,
And like a pack-horse tires without his bells.
Their fancies like our bushy-points° appear;
The poets tag them, we for fashion wear.   50

39 bird . . . Paradise The bird of Paradise was supposed to have
no feet and to remain in perpetual flight.   **43 Tiresias** the blind
prophet of Thebes.   **46 rhyme** Dryden's *State of Innocence* is in
heroic couplets. Milton is said to have given Dryden permission
to "tag his verses."   **47 Town-Bayes** Buckingham's *Rehearsal* (1672)
presented Dryden as Bayes, and the nickname stuck.   **49 bushy-
points** for fastening hose; the ends were often tasselled. He means
that whereas we use such frivolous ornaments only for "fashion,"
such poets as Dryden employ them (viz., rhymes) as necessary to
their halting verses.

I too transported by the mode offend,
And while I meant to *praise* thee, must *commend*.°
Thy verse created like thy theme sublime,
In number, weight, and measure,° needs not rhyme.

51–52 I ... commend Caught up in this fashion, I can't use the
word "praise" but must say "commend" for the sake of the rhyme.
54 number ... measure *Wisdom*, xi, 20.

Index of First Lines

THE SIGNET CLASSIC POETRY SERIES presents, in inexpensive format, comprehensive, authoritative, and up-to-date editions of the works of the major British and American poets. Prepared under the general editorship of John Hollander, Professor of English at Hunter College, each volume in the series is devoted to a single poet, and edited by a noted scholar. Included in each volume is an introduction by the individual editor, a bibliography, a textual note, and detailed footnotes.

SAMSON AGONISTES AND THE SHORTER POEMS OF JOHN MILTON

Edited with Introduction by Isabel Gamble MacCaffrey
L'Allegro, Il Penseroso, Lycidas, a selection of the sonnets, and many other important poems, with an informative introduction by an Associate Professor at Bryn Mawr College and author of *Paradise Lost as a Myth.*
(CT323—75¢)

SELECTED POETRY AND PROSE OF BYRON

Edited with Introduction by W. H. Auden
A comprehensive selection of the works of the great nineteenth century poet, including selections from *Don Juan, Childe Harold, English Bards* and *Scotch Reviewers,* extracts from the *Journal* of 1816 and the Diary of 1821, and much more. (CQ346—95¢)

SELECTED POETRY OF DONNE

Edited with Introduction by Marius Bewley
The complete "Songs and Sonnets," "Elegies," "Epithalamions," "Satyres," and many other works of the great metaphysical poet who has gained new popularity during the twentieth century. (CQ343—95¢)

SELECTED POETRY OF KEATS

Edited with Introduction by Paul de Man
A rich sampling of the Romantic poet's works, arranged chronologically, including the complete "Endymion" and "Hyperion," as well as many of the shorter poetical works and a selection of the letters.
(CQ325—95¢)

SELECTED POETRY OF SHELLEY

Edited with Introduction by Harold Bloom
The complete text of the lyrical drama, "Prometheus Bound," plus such well-known poems as "Ozymandias," "Ode to the West Wind," "To a Skylark," "Adonais," and many others, and two important prose selections, "On a Future State" and "Defense of Poetry."
(CQ342—95¢)

The SIGNET CLASSIC SHAKESPEARE

Superlatively edited paperbound volumes of the complete works of Shakespeare are now being added to the Signet Classic list. Under the general editorship of Sylvan Barnet, Chairman of the English Department of Tufts University, each volume features a general Introduction by Dr. Barnet; special Introduction and Notes by an eminent Shakespearean scholar; critical commentary from past and contemporary authorities, and when possible, the original source material, in its entirety or in excerpt, on which Shakespeare based his work. Among the titles already available, at 50¢ each, are: